TWO FOR THE
PRICE OF ONE!

Fury saw that the two men were lined up just right and took advantage of the opportunity. He tipped up the barrel of the Sharps and squeezed the trigger. It was a daring, almost foolhardy, maneuver, and Fury knew it. The recoil almost wrenched Fury's hand off, but the .50 caliber ball entered the belly of the first man, ripped through his vitals, then burst out his back to catch the second man in the chest. . . .

FURY

LAST CHANCE CANYON

JIM AUSTIN

BERKLEY BOOKS, NEW YORK

LAST CHANCE CANYON

A Berkley Book / published by arrangement with
the author

PRINTING HISTORY
Berkley edition / July 1993

ISBN: 0-425-13810-0

A BERKLEY BOOK ® TM 757,375
Berkley Books are published by The Berkley Publishing Group,
200 Madison Avenue, New York, New York 10016.
The name "BERKLEY" and the "B" logo
are trademarks belonging to Berkley Publishing Corporation.

PRINTED IN THE UNITED STATES OF AMERICA

10 9 8 7 6 5 4 3 2 1

For Len Meares,
with great respect

CHAPTER
1

....

Fury was in the high country, slanting along a ridge overlooking the American River, when he found the gut-shot man.

With a smooth tug on the reins, Fury brought his big dun horse to a halt as a moan of agony came drifting out of the brush to the right of the trail. His right hand went to the well-worn walnut butt of the Colt's Third Model Dragoon holstered on his hip. This was rough country. A man who wasn't careful could walk into a trap, and anybody who was too quick to play the good samaritan could get his damn fool head blown off real easy.

If the man in the brush was faking, he was doing a mighty fine job of it, Fury decided after a moment. He swung down from the saddle, drew the heavy revolver, and stepped into the thick growth that lined the faint path.

It was spring, and the trees and bushes were budding and spreading greenery over these hills and mountainsides. Fury had money in his poke, plenty of supplies on the pack mule trailing behind the dun, and no reason at all to go sticking his nose into other folks' troubles. Old habits were hard to break, he supposed, as he carefully pushed some brush aside and saw the bloody form writhing feebly on the ground.

Still might be a trap, Fury thought, but the hurt looked genuine enough. Looked like the boy had taken at least two slugs in the belly, which had to have torn him up inside something awful. Fury shouldered through the growth into the little clearing and knelt beside the moaning youngster.

"Rest easy," Fury said as he laid his left hand on the boy's shoulder.

The boy jerked at the touch, opened his eyes, and looked up at Fury. "M-mister!" he gasped. "They . . . shot me! Just up an' . . . shot me!"

"I can see that," Fury told him quietly. "Now, you lay still as you can. Rolling around's liable to make it hurt worse."

Fury lifted his head, looked around, and listened intently. He could hear birds singing and small animals moving through the brush, along with the occasional stamp and snort of his horse and mule. He sniffed. No smell of burned powder in the air. All of that told him the shooting had taken place a while back, long enough for the smoke to blow away and things to settle down again. Chances were whoever had done this was already a long way off.

Fury holstered his gun and then gently pulled aside the bloodstained shirt until he could see the pair of ugly holes in the boy's stomach. The boy was watching him, so he tried to keep what he saw from showing on his face. He asked, "How old are you, son?"

"T-twenty. . . ."

"And what's your name?"

"J-Johnny Ph-Phipps. . . ."

"My name's John, too. John Fury."

Somehow the boy managed to smile a little. "P-pleased to meet you . . . Mr. Fury. . . . There . . . there ain't nothin' you can . . . do for me . . . is there?"

"I reckon you must know you're hurt pretty bad. It's still forty miles or more to San Francisco. You'd never make it that far. Is there a doctor closer that you know of?"

Johnny Phipps's head moved slowly from side to side. "I don't figure . . . I could make it a mile, Mr. Fury . . . even if there was a sawbones. . . . You got any . . . whiskey?"

"A little, but that'll just make it hurt more," Fury warned.

"Don't care. I got to . . . tell you some things . . . 'fore it's too late."

Seeing the determination on the boy's face, Fury nodded.

"I'll be right back," he promised.

He stood up and went quickly back to the trail, hoping that Johnny Phipps wouldn't be dead by the time he returned. He took a small flask of whiskey from his saddlebag and pushed back through the brush.

The boy was still alive. Fury knelt beside him again, lifted his head, trickled what was left of the whiskey into his mouth. Johnny closed his eyes, shuddered, and turned even paler, although Fury would not have thought that was possible. But then a little color came back into the youngster's face, and his voice was a bit stronger when he opened his eyes and spoke again.

"There was three of 'em jumped me," he said. "I was carryin' the mail, and I reckon they thought I might have some . . . gold dust or money in some of the letters."

"Express rider, are you?"

Johnny Phipps shook his head. "Not usually. That's my . . . my brother's job. We . . . we come out here to get rich in the gold fields."

You and a hundred thousand more just like you, Fury thought.

"Milo . . . that's my brother . . . he went to work for Mr. Todd in San Francisco . . . bringin' in letters from the miners and carryin' back any mail they had comin' to 'em. But he was sick, and I said I'd take care of this run for him. Then those . . . bastards jumped me, took the mail pouch." Johnny closed his eyes again. "Reckon I let ol' Milo down. But I tried to get the mail back. That's when they . . . when they shot me." He chuckled, then winced as a fresh spasm of pain went through him. "Never figured anybody would . . . shoot somebody over some . . . mail."

"I'm sorry, kid," Fury said. "Some men are just trigger-happy, I guess."

But Johnny Phipps wasn't listening to him anymore. The boy's sky-blue eyes were staring straight up and beginning to glaze over.

The lines of agony etched in the young man's face smoothed

out, leaving him looking sort of peaceful, a gangling, sandy-haired kid who should have been walking behind a mule and a plow somewhere instead of lying there dead and bloody in the California mountains. Fury sighed, gently lowered the boy's head, and stood up.

Rage smoldered inside him. He didn't know if Johnny Phipps had actually been carrying any valuables or not in that mail sack. But it didn't matter. The young, temporary express rider had been cut down just on the chance that there might be some gold dust or money to be gained by his death. Any man who would do something like that was just a vulture in human form as far as Fury was concerned. Hell, worse than a vulture!

Fury took a deep breath and calmed himself. There was nothing he could do about Johnny Phipps's murder. The men responsible for it were long gone. At least the boy hadn't died out here by himself, and he wouldn't have to lie here until the wolves got him. Fury would see that he was buried decent.

There was a shovel tied on with the other gear on the pack mule. Fury went to get it.

He wasn't heading any place in particular and was in no hurry to get there, so after he had dug the grave, wrapped Johnny Phipps's body in one of his blankets, lowered it into the ground, and filled in the dirt, he used his ax to hack down a sapling and make a marker, smoothing the crosspiece enough so that he could carve Johnny's name into it with his Bowie knife. Unsure when the boy had been born, as well as what today's date was, Fury left it at that.

He scouted around, decided that the horse Johnny must have been riding was no longer in the vicinity, and then paused one final time beside the grave.

"Sorry you had to come to an end like this, son. If I get to San Francisco, I'll try to look up that Todd fella you mentioned and let him know what happened, so that he can tell your brother. Maybe that'll help you rest a mite easier."

There was nothing else to say. Fury had never been much of a praying man. He put on his wide-brimmed, flat-crowned black hat and went back to his animals.

The afternoon had gotten warm, especially with all the digging he'd done, and his faded blue work shirt was dark with sweat. What he needed now was a drink, and he hoped to hell he could find one somewhere this side of San Francisco.

The rugged mountains of the Sierra Nevada seemed isolated and uninhabited at first glance, but that was deceptive. There were roads and trails here, and far-flung plumes of smoke climbed into the sky to mark settlements or in some places just single cabins or tents. Several years earlier, back in '48, a trader named Sutter had hired a carpenter to build a sawmill for him. The carpenter, James Marshall, had gone poking around in the American River instead of sticking to his lumber and nails, and he had found something that had changed this part of the world for good and all.

Something yellow and shiny. . . .

The gold rush had done more than just attract hundreds of thousands of men to California in search of their fortunes. It had caught the fancy of the country as well, and from one end of the nation to the other, journalists had written of gold and its irresistible lure. People seemed to think there was something glamorous and romantic about chipping away at a hillside with a pick and shovel or squatting beside a stream with a pan for hours on end or rocking a sluice from dawn to dark.

Those who were there knew better. They knew how mining sapped a man's strength and made his muscles scream for relief. They knew how frustration grew as the long, tedious days passed with no sign of color. The lucky ones might make a fortune, and the ones who were lucky *and* smart might even manage to hang on to some of their riches, but for the overwhelming majority of the men who had swarmed into California after the discovery at Sutter's Mill, the only payoff had been failure . . . and sometimes death.

But that didn't stop them from coming. Unless all the gold in the whole state played out, ambitious men would keep leaving their farms and families behind and heading for the hills.

Gold in California! It was a siren call that could not be denied.

The crudely carved signpost read SAN FRANSISKO 40 MIELS, and an arrow burned into the wood underneath the letters pointed along the trail leading southwest. The road Fury had been following intersected the San Francisco trail, and as he reined in to look at the sign, he heard a burst of laughter coming through the open door of a trading post across the way. It was the only building in sight, and the sign above its door proclaimed it to be the NARWHALE TRADDING POST AND SALLOON. Fury figured the man who owned it was probably the same one who had put up the signpost.

He turned the dun's head and heeled it into motion, leading the pack mule along behind. There were four horses tied up at the hitch rack in front of the trading post. All of the animals looked tired and hard-ridden, and one of the saddles had a dark brown splotch on it that Fury recognized as blood.

He tied the dun and the pack mule and went up four steps onto the plank porch. The raucous laughter was still coming from inside the trading post.

The sun had dipped below the western horizon about ten minutes earlier; it was a bad time of day to be walking into a strange place. There were a couple of lanterns lit, but their chimneys were so smoky that they didn't give off much light. Fury paused just inside the door to let his eyes adjust and hoped he didn't have any old enemies waiting for him in there.

Such things had happened before, more often than he liked to think about.

Nobody paid any attention to him this time, though. Shelves loaded down with pots and pans, picks and shovels, bolts of the dyed canvas sailcloth made popular by a San Francisco tailor named Levi Strauss, canteens, tent pegs, and just about everything else a man would need to outfit himself for some prospecting stretched out to both sides of the trading post's entrance. About halfway to the rear of the building, a counter jutted out from the left-hand wall and then curved around to form a bar for the saloon that occupied the right rear corner. That was where the noise was coming from.

Three men were sitting at a table and passing around a bottle of whiskey, probably homemade stuff brewed up in a barrel out behind the trading post. One of the men had a young woman sitting on his lap, and as he used one hand to tilt the bottle to his lips, the other came up to pinch a full breast through the woman's thin blouse. She flinched a little at the rough caress, but the smile on her lips never wavered and she made no move to get up. Her hair was a tangled mass of reddish-blond curls, and while she wasn't pretty, she was certainly ripe. That was all the three customers cared about.

None of the men even glanced at Fury as he walked to the bar and nodded to the man and woman standing behind it. The man said, "Greetings to ye. What'll ye have?"

"Beer, if you've got it," Fury replied.

"Oh, aye, that we do," the man said. He picked up a small bucket and began filling it from a keg.

The woman leaned on the bar, offering Fury a smile and a look down the pale valley of her sizable bosom. Her hair was the same color as the younger woman's, and Fury figured them for mother and daughter.

The bartender put the bucket of beer on the counter and said, "That'll be two bits."

Fury dropped a coin on the bar, picked up the beer, and went to one of the half-dozen empty tables. He sat down so that he could keep an eye on both the doorway and the table where the other men were sitting and pawing the young woman. He sampled the beer. It was warm and bitter, but he knew it was probably better than the panther piss the other men were drinking.

He was aware of the bartender watching him, and after a few minutes, the man's curiosity got the better of him. He limped out from behind the counter and came toward Fury, the wooden peg in which his right leg ended thumping against the planks of the floor as he came. He gestured toward one of the empty chairs at the table and asked, "Ye mind if I sit?"

"Help yourself." Fury shrugged. "It's your place."

"Aye, that it is. Benjamin Ross, that's me name."

The man didn't ask for Fury's name, and Fury didn't volunteer it.

Ross went on. "Ye don't look like most o' the men who come in here."

"How's that?" Fury asked.

"Desperate to find gold. I was that way meself once, so I know how they feel. They got the cravin' so bad, you can almost smell it on 'em, like a horse that's been run all day."

Fury shook his head. "I'm not looking for gold," he admitted. "Just passing through."

Ross put his hands on his knees and stretched out the leg that ended in a wooden peg, easing it. After a moment, he said, "Ye're probably wonderin' about the name o' this place."

"Nope. Figured you for a whaler, probably from up around Alaska way. Mighty cold waters up there, where the narwhales are found."

Ross's face lit up. "Ye're a seagoin' man yerself?"

"Now and then. A long time back. And I wouldn't ship out again for all the gold in the Sierra Nevada."

"I feel the same way," Ross said fervently. He slapped his bad leg. "Harpoon cable got wrapped around me foot by accident one day. Damn whale sounded and pinched the foot right off. I swore right then an' there that if I lived to tell the tale, I'd never set foot—or peg leg—on a deck again." Ross laughed. "And I ain't, right enough! But I got some good memories o' them days, too, an' that's why I called this place the Narwhale."

Fury swallowed some more beer and grinned. "I was lucky, I reckon. I got back to shore in one piece and didn't figure to press my luck."

"Well, if there's anything else ye need, anything at all, ye just let me know."

"Got a room I could rent for the night?"

"Aye. Rooms in the back, four bits a night." Ross inclined

his head toward the other customers. "Those gents ain't said whether they're stayin' or not."

Fury shook his head. "Doesn't matter to me one way or the other what they do." He handed Ross a dollar. "That's for the room and a couple more buckets of beer."

"Aye. I'll bring 'em when ye're needin' 'em."

The man limped back to the bar and spoke in a low voice to the woman. In the meantime, Fury looked over at the girl and saw that she bore a resemblance to Ross as well. The trading post was obviously a family operation.

A slight frown creased Fury's brow. There were four horses tied up outside, but he had only seen three customers in here. All of the horses had worn saddles, so one of them wasn't a pack animal.

Where was the fourth man? And was his horse the one with blood on the saddle?

Fury didn't have any answers for those questions, but he couldn't help wondering about them.

A few minutes later, the woman from behind the bar brought over another bucket of beer, even though Fury hadn't quite finished the first one. Ross had gone back around the corner into the area that served as the trading post, and Fury could no longer see him. The woman set the beer down on the table and smiled at Fury again.

"Ben told me to bring this over to you," she said. "He told me to treat you nice, too, since you've been to sea."

"A long time ago," Fury told her, just as he had told her husband.

"That doesn't matter to Ben. He never has gotten used to being back on land, no matter what he says." She shrugged. "But he's too old and crippled up to sail anymore. That's the real reason he's here."

There was nothing to say to that, so Fury kept quiet. After a few seconds, the woman sat down without being asked. She hitched her chair closer to Fury's.

"I know I'm not as young as my daughter," she said in a low voice. "But I can still show you a mighty good time, mister."

Her hand dropped to Fury's thigh under the table.

"What about Ben?" Fury asked tightly.

"Oh, he doesn't care." The woman gave a little laugh. "Hell, you know those old sailors. They'll share anything with you if they like you."

Fury shook his head, hoping she wouldn't be insulted by his answer. "I don't think so," he said. "I'm a mite tired. Rode a long way today."

The woman shrugged. "Sure, I understand. Not that I'm not a little disappointed. But I guess I can help Sarah out with those other gents." She stood up, smiled again, and sauntered toward the table where the other men sat.

Fury drank his beer and looked past her at the three men. The girl had been handed over to another lap, and she had her arms curled around the neck of a man with a bushy black beard. He guffawed and said, "I tell you, boys, nothin' makes me itch for a woman like a shootin'."

"Hush up, Judd," one of the other men said. "You'll scare that little darlin', make her think we're some sort o' bad men."

"Hell, we are, ain't we?" Judd demanded. "Didn't we just—"

"Shut up," snapped the third man. "If you can't keep your big mouth shut, then at least stick a whiskey bottle in it so's we don't have to hear you talk."

Judd glared and pushed the girl off his lap. She gave a small cry of surprise and caught her balance before she fell to the floor. Her mother hurried forward and took her arm. "Here now!" the older woman scolded. "You treat my little girl decent, mister."

"Lady, I'm goin' to treat her so decent she won't be able to walk come mornin'," Judd said, then turned his attention back to his companion. "You got no right to say such things to me as you just did, Frank. It ain't my fault that feller weren't carryin' no money."

Fury took another swallow of beer. It didn't do a thing to calm the hammering that had suddenly started in his head.

The third man reached down to the floor at his feet and picked up something. He tossed it on the table and laughed. "How many more bottles o' whiskey'll that fetch?" he asked Ross's wife.

The thing on the table was a leather pouch, a good-sized one.

Just the sort of thing a man would use to carry mail.

CHAPTER
2

Fury sat where he was for a few minutes longer, even though he was sure the three men were the ones who had ambushed Johnny Phipps, gut-shot him, and left him to die in agony in the brush alongside the trail. During that time, the bandits known as Judd and Frank glowered at each other some more, then put aside their differences and pulled the Ross women back onto their laps.

"Hell, I ain't in no mood to fight." Judd laughed. "I'd rather do some lovin' instead."

The older woman perched on his knee and picked up the leather pouch from the table. "This is mighty nice," she said. "I reckon Ben'd trade you a few bottles for it. But where'd you come by it?"

Fury got to his feet and said grimly, "They stole it."

That threw cold water on the celebration. All three men jerked their heads around to stare at him in surprise, and the women looked, too.

Fury went on. "They stole it from a twenty-year-old kid after they shot him twice in the belly. That's the kind of men you're being nice to now, Mrs. Ross."

"That's a goddamned lie," Frank said. He stood up, dumping the daughter. Fury kept a close eye on him. The man hadn't made a move toward his gun . . . yet.

Mrs. Ross stood up and reached for the pouch, a worried look on her round face. "That *does* look a little like the pouch the Phipps boy was carrying the last time he came by here."

13

She started to turn, calling "Ben!" as she did so.

Suddenly, Judd came up out of his chair, grabbing the woman's arm and giving her a hard shove that sent her stumbling straight toward Fury. At the same time, he yanked his pistol out of its holster.

Fury bit back a curse. With Mrs. Ross between him and the men, not to mention the younger woman just scrambling back to her feet beside the table, he couldn't just pull his Colt and start thumbing off shots. He had to dart forward, grab the shoulder of the staggering woman, and fling her out of the way.

Judd's gun roared and the woman screamed. The bullet had grazed her left shoulder, but it would have plowed into the back of her neck if Fury hadn't knocked her aside. It whipped on past Fury, barely missing him before thudding into the wall behind him.

Frank and the other man were reaching for their guns, but Judd was the only one with a weapon drawn, so Fury took him first. The Dragoon boomed heavily, smoke and flame belching from its muzzle. The .44 caliber ball slammed into Judd's broad chest, driving him back against the table, which tipped over and then was smashed into kindling when he fell on it.

Fury was already thumbing back the hammer for a second shot before Frank's gun cleared leather. Fury didn't wait. He squeezed the trigger, and the crash of the Dragoon again filled the air. The shot caught Frank in the right elbow, smashing the bones to powder and nearly blowing the arm clean in two. Frank spun around, howling in agony.

The third man got a shot off, but it went wild over Fury's head. Fury switched his aim and fired twice this time, both balls going into the man's belly and folding him up like a house of cards. He hit the floor and started to squirm and howl.

Fury took a deep breath. He had no idea which of the three had actually pulled the trigger on Johnny Phipps—probably all of them, knowing how road agents like that operated—but those last two shots had been for Johnny, anyway.

Ross stumped hurriedly back around the corner and ran to his wife and daughter as Fury stepped over to the three robbers. With a booted foot, he kicked the guns away from their sprawled bodies, holding the big Colt cocked and ready just in case any of them wanted to try anything else. But Judd was dead, Frank was passed out cold from shock and loss of blood, and the other man was out of his head from the pain of having a couple of holes blown through his guts. Fury toed him over onto his back and looked down at his twisted face.

"Goddamn!" Benjamin Ross said in an awed whisper. "Goddamn! I never seen anything like . . . Who the hell *are* you, mister?"

Fury ignored the question as he reloaded the chambers he had fired and slid the revolver back into its holster. The third man let out another moan and then fell silent as unconsciousness mercifully claimed him, too. His whole midsection was sodden with blood, and Fury knew he wouldn't be waking up.

"How's your wife?" Fury asked as he turned back to Ross. The woman was still whimpering in pain and the shoulder of her dress was torn, but as her daughter finished ripping the fabric away from the wound, Fury saw that it was only a red welt, a bullet burn. Hurt like the devil but didn't amount to much, he knew from experience.

"She'll be all right," Ross said after glancing at the wound. "But what I want to know is why you killed those men."

"They held up an express rider earlier today, young fella named Johnny Phipps. Killed him for what was in that pouch." Fury gestured toward the leather bag, which was lying on the floor in the rubble of the collapsed table, next to Judd's body.

"Phipps. . . ." Ross rubbed his bulldog jaw in thought. "Aye, that's the name o' the lad who carries the mail through these parts. Killed him, you say?"

Fury nodded.

"Then the scurvy bastards got what was comin' to 'em," Ross declared. "I never seen 'em before, but I knew they was bad ones as soon as they come in. There's a deep ravine out back. I'll haul 'em out there and toss 'em in."

"Got any law in these parts you need to notify?"

Ross snorted. "Hell, there ain't hardly any law in San Francisco, let alone this far from town. I don't reckon anybody'll miss those men, or think bad of me for throwin' 'em in the gully."

"Sounds like the best place for them," Fury grunted. He bent and picked up the mail pouch, able to tell from the weight of it that there was still something in it. He unfastened the buckle that held it closed and took out a handful of envelopes and folded sheets of paper, most of them covered with crudely printed writing. The letters had been jumbled and crumpled in disgust by the robbers when they found that their efforts hadn't netted them any payoff, but at least they hadn't dumped the mail and let the wind blow it away.

"What're ye goin' to do with that?" Ross asked, pointing at the pouch.

Fury wasn't sure where the words came from, but he said, "I'm going to take it on to San Francisco and deliver it, just like that young fella would have done if they hadn't killed him." Maybe it was just a whim, but he meant the promise.

Ross's wife spoke up, saying, "I don't figure anybody's going to argue with you, mister, not after what you just did."

He was used to the look they were giving him. It was the expression most people wore after they'd seen him use his gun. It was a combination of almost equal parts admiration and utter fear. Law-abiding folks had no reason to be scared of him, but usually it was too complicated to explain that. So he just went on his way and left them to talk about him, and that was the way the stories grew up. Fury didn't much like it, but there was nothing he could do about it.

Ross bent, grabbed one of the corpses by the feet, and started dragging him out. Fury saw that both of the wounded men, Frank and the other one, were dead now, having succumbed to their injuries.

"You could stay for a while," the daughter said, hunger in her eyes. "You can't ride on in to San Francisco tonight. And you've already paid for your room. Ain't that right, Ma?"

"That's right," the woman agreed. "You'd best stay."

"All right," Fury said with a nod. "Reckon there'll be plenty of room."

"More'n enough," the girl purred, sidling over to take his arm.

"I'll stay," Fury said, "alone."

She pouted in disappointment, but Fury wasn't going to change his mind. The death of Johnny Phipps and then the gunfight with his killers had blunted any thoughts Fury might have had of female companionship. Right now, all he wanted was some whiskey, even if it was homemade rotgut, and a place to sleep.

He slung the mail pouch over his shoulder, leaned over to the bar to snag a bottle, then said to Mrs. Ross, "Your husband said something about rooms in the back . . . ?"

She sighed, just as disappointed as her daughter, and said, "I'll show you."

The bed in the narrow little room was lumpy and uncomfortable, but Fury slept soundly anyway—as soundly, at least, as he ever slept. He was up early the next morning, and Mrs. Ross fed him flapjacks that were almost as lumpy as the bed. Then he followed the one-legged former sailor outside.

"What about the horses those gents rode in on?" Ross asked, nodding toward the small corral where he had put the animals the night before.

"I want the one that was carrying a bloodstained saddle," Fury said. "Reckon that was the one Phipps was riding, and it belonged either to him or to the express company, I'm not sure which. But I'll take it on in to the city and turn it over

to the man Phipps worked for." With a shrug, Fury went on.
"I don't care what you do with the other three. Sell 'em and
keep the money if you want."

"Yeah, maybe I'll do that. That'll help pay for the table
that got all busted up when that fella landed on it."

With a little profit to boot, Fury thought, but he didn't say
anything. He had enough of a stake at the moment; he wasn't
interested in the money that the thieves' horses might bring.

As Fury was saddling the dun, he said, "Thanks for taking
care of this old boy. He can be sort of cantankerous at times.
Hope he didn't nip you."

"We got along just fine," Ross replied. He glanced at the
building, where the two women were standing in the rear door
and watching them. "Sure ye got to be movin' on? I know me
womenfolk wouldn't mind if ye stayed another day or two."

"Got to deliver this mail," Fury said as he slung the pouch
across the dun's back along with his own saddlebags. Then
he got his gear loaded on the pack mule and when that was
done swung up into his saddle. "So long, Ross." He touched
a finger to the brim of his hat and nodded at the women.
"Ladies."

The daughter called after him, "If you ever come back this
way, you better stop!"

Fury rode on without looking back, leading the pack mule
and Johnny Phipps's horse.

Fury was glad he hadn't told them his name. He had kept
that information to himself.

But word of what had happened would still get around,
and for the sake of less trouble in the future, he hoped those
three robbers didn't have any kin who might come looking
for him, hoping to settle the score for their dead relatives.
That had happened too often in the past, too. Fury supposed
it was what came of having to shoot more people than he
really would have preferred. . . .

Leading the two animals like that, the forty miles between
the Narwhale Trading Post and San Francisco took him two

full days to cover. It was after nightfall of the second day when he found himself riding down Pacific Avenue, one of the main streets of the city by the bay. He and the horses and the mule had taken the ferry across San Francisco Bay, past the humpbacked shapes of Goat Island and Angel Island. Lights were burning in the mansions on Nob Hill, rising on Fury's left as he headed down the avenue. To his right was Telegraph Hill, with the Italian community known as North Beach on its western slope. Up ahead was the hilarity of Kearny Street and Portsmouth Square, but before Fury reached that part of town, he paused in the business district, wondering if he would find Alexander Todd at his office at this time of night.

Reining in and hailing a passerby who seemed sober enough to answer a question, Fury asked him where the express company's office might be found.

"Turn left here on Montgomery Street," the man told Fury. "Todd's offices are in the Brink Building, along with Wells, Fargo."

Fury nodded his thanks and rode on, and when he reached the building, sure enough there were lights burning in its windows. Maybe he was going to be lucky after all.

He tied the two horses and the mule to a hitch rack in front of the building and went to the front door, which had a sign on it that read TODD'S EXPRESS AND BANKING OFFICES. It was locked, but when Fury rapped sharply on it, a shape appeared after a moment, silhouetted against the shade drawn down over the door. The shade was moved aside slightly, and a man holding a lantern peered out. "What is it?" he called. "We're closed!"

Fury held up the mail pouch so that the man could see it in the light that came through the glass. "I think this belongs to you," he said, raising his voice enough for the man to hear him through the door.

The man's eyes widened in surprise, and he reached down quickly to twist the key in the lock. As he swung the door open, he stepped back and said in accusing tones, "That's the bag Johnny Phipps was carrying. He should have been back yesterday."

"I know," Fury said as he stepped into the office. "Never said it wasn't. Are you Todd?"

The man was slender and younger than Fury had expected, probably still in his twenties, although the dark, drooping mustache made him look slightly older. "I'm Alexander Todd," he confirmed. "And you are . . . ?"

"Name's John Fury." He tossed the pouch on a nearby desk. "Some robbers held up your man Phipps about fifty miles back up in the mountains, shot him and stole his horse and the pouch."

"Good Lord!" Alexander Todd exclaimed. "Is he—"

"Dead," Fury said with a nod. "I'm afraid so. But so are the men who jumped him. I came along before the boy died, and he told me what happened. I caught up to them a while after I'd buried Phipps."

"And you confronted them?"

Fury nodded.

"Are you some sort of lawman?" Todd wanted to know.

"Nope. Just a man who doesn't like the kind of hombre who'd gut-shoot a youngster and then leave him there to die." Fury gestured at the leather pouch. "Reckon it was just sort of accidental that I recovered the mail for you, but once I had it, made sense to bring it on in."

"I'm grateful to you, Mr. Fury." Todd picked up the pouch and opened it, began pawing through the jumbled contents. "Not just for bringing this pouch to me, but for seeing that young Phipps was buried decently. *And* for avenging his death. I'd like to offer you something for your trouble. . . ."

"Didn't do it for any reward," Fury said curtly.

"Oh, I understand that. But you deserve *some* compensation." An idea lit up Todd's face. "Would you be interested in a job?"

"A job?" Fury repeated, surprised. "What kind of job?"

"Delivering the mail, of course."

Fury grinned and shook his head. "Never figured myself the sort to be delivering mail. This was a special case."

"But it can be quite lucrative, especially carrying letters back out to the gold camps." Todd paused, then went on. "I charge an ounce of gold dust for every letter delivered—and there are usually enough sacks of outgoing mail to require a pack animal to carry them."

Fury let out a low whistle. Gold dust was worth about sixteen dollars an ounce, and you could probably put several hundred letters in a sack big enough to be carried on a pack mule. Load one on each side of the mule and . . .

"That's a lot of money," Fury admitted.

"So you see, I can afford to pay my carriers quite well. I wish you'd give my offer some thought, Mr. Fury. I need men such as yourself, who can deal with the dangers of a rugged land and even rougher men."

"Instead of boys like Johnny Phipps," Fury commented.

"I have to hire whoever I can get," Todd said with a shrug. "Most of the men around here don't want to be tied down to a steady job. They're too interested in looking for gold dust themselves. I hired Milo Phipps, young Johnny's brother, after he had given up on prospecting. Johnny was just filling in for him while Milo recuperates from a bad case of the grippe." Todd frowned and shook his head. "I suppose I'll have to tell Milo about Johnny's death. I don't look forward to that chore."

"Better you than me," Fury said. "Reckon I'll be going now."

"Wait, Mr. Fury. What about the job?"

"I'll think on it," Fury promised. "Phipps's horse is tied up outside. Was it his, or did it belong to your company?"

"It was his personal mount," Todd answered. "I'll see that Milo gets it, along with the wages Johnny had coming to him."

"You do that," Fury said. With a brusque nod, he left the office.

He had kept the vow he had made back there at Ross's trading post, he mused, as he rode on toward Portsmouth Square. The mail pouch had been delivered, along with the news of Johnny Phipps's death. All three of the robbers had had justice meted out to them. Fury could put this whole episode behind him now and get on with his drifting.

But somehow, he thought, things hardly ever worked out that way. . . .

CHAPTER
3

....

In 1848, when Fury laid eyes on San Francisco for the first time, the settlement was nothing but a sleepy little seacoast town of around eight hundred people, despite the fact that it was the only natural port for hundreds of miles up and down the Pacific Coast. Only in recent months had its name been changed from Yerba Buena to San Francisco, following the American victory in the war against Mexico that had been responsible for all of California becoming part of the United States.

Then had come the discovery of gold, and now, less than a decade later, well over a hundred thousand people called San Francisco home. It was the largest city Fury had visited in quite some time, and he felt a little uncomfortable here. A man got used to open air around him, rather than a bunch of buildings, some of them towering four or five stories.

Fury rode into Portsmouth Square, and from the looks of the crowd in the area, it seemed as if half the town was here getting drunk. The numerous saloons around the square were doing a booming business. He angled the dun toward one called the Lucky Nugget. There had probably been some wishful thinking on the part of the place's owner in selecting that name, Fury thought.

The hitch rack was crowded, but he found a place to tie the dun and the pack mule. Fury slung his saddlebags over his shoulder and slid the Sharps .50 caliber carbine from the saddleboot and tucked it under his left arm. He wasn't worried about somebody stealing the animals or the provisions, but he didn't want to tempt anybody by leaving anything else behind.

From what he had heard, crime here in San Francisco wasn't as bad as it used to be, mainly because the vigilance committees had strung up a few thieves and killers and put the fear of God into most of the would-be lawbreakers. The Hounds, a gang from New York, had been run out of town, as had the Sydney Ducks, another bad bunch comprised of immigrants from Australia. The vigilance committees had disbanded now, but they could form up again quickly enough if there was another outbreak of lawlessness.

Fury stepped into the Lucky Nugget, eyes stinging from the thick haze of cigar smoke and ears ringing from the noise that filled the air along with the smoke. In one corner of the room, a slick-haired gent in sleeve gaiters was pounding on a piano, while in another a trio of Mexicans were strumming guitars and singing songs that were old when the grandees were still running things around here. Men shouted at one another, and bursts of raucous laughter came from the mob at the long mahogany bar. Booted feet stomped the dance floor as miners and sailors and adventurers of every stripe moved awkwardly around with spangle-wearing gals in their arms. The click of a roulette wheel and the soft whisper of cards being dealt onto baize tabletops served only as a faint counterpoint to the louder noises. In short, the same sort of good-natured chaos filled this saloon as could be found in all the other establishments in Portsmouth Square.

Shouldering his way toward the bar, Fury was the recipient of more than one drunken, belligerent glance from the men he passed. No one was willing to take too much offense at being bumped, though, not once they got a good look at him. They saw a husky, formidable-looking man in his thirties, wearing a black hat, blue work shirt, buckskin pants, and high-topped boots, all of which had seen a lot of hard wear.

What made the men hesitate before saying anything, however, was the Colt, the Sharps, and the Bowie, which were
as well-used as the rest of Fury's outfit.

When he reached the bar, Fury nodded to the sweat-
ing bartender on the other side of the hardwood. Like
the piano player, the man wore a vest and sleeve gaiters. He had wispy grayish-brown hair and the look of a
mournful hound dog on his long face. Lifting his voice
to be heard over the din, he asked, "What can I get
you, Slim?" From the sound of it, he addressed everyone
like that.

"Whiskey," Fury told him as he placed his saddlebags on
the mahogany and leaned the carbine against the bar, "and
then beer after that."

The bartender nodded, splashed amber liquid into a glass
from a bottle, then slid it across to Fury and started filling a
mug from a beer keg almost in the same motion. Fury admired
the smooth efficiency with which he worked. Handing the
man a five-dollar gold piece, Fury said, "I'll drink my way
through that."

"You're the boss."

Fury leaned an elbow on the hardwood, tossed back
the whiskey, then reached for the beer. As he did so,
he looked up and down the bar. It was long, running
nearly the whole length of the saloon's left-hand wall,
and there were four bartenders working behind it. From
the looks of things, all four of them were kept busy
by the Lucky Nugget's customers. The one closest to
Fury, other than the man who had served him drinks,
was a burly, bullet-headed gent who looked not only out
of place but uncomfortable in his white shirt and bro-
caded vest. There was a surly expression on his flor-
id face.

"Things always this busy?" Fury asked the first bartender.

"This ain't busy, Slim," the man said in his husky voice,
reaching under the bar to bring out a smoldering quirly and
take a drag on it. "On a busy night, I don't even get to breathe,

let alone smoke." His solemn expression didn't change as he spoke in a dry tone of voice.

Fury grinned across the bar at him. "Do you get a chance to have a drink yourself?" he asked.

"Oh, now and then, now and then." He put the quirly back under the bar and then extended his hand to Fury. "Name's Hoagland."

"John Fury."

Hoagland had a good grip, and Fury felt an instinctive liking for him. Fury went on. "Have one on me, and take it out of that five dollars."

"You sure about that, John?"

"I'm sure."

Hoagland reached for another mug. "Thanks. I'll make it beer, if you don't mind, since I'm working."

"That's fine," Fury assured him. While Hoagland was drawing the beer for himself, Fury turned halfway around, enough to survey the crowded room. Men were jostling him on both sides, and he didn't much like the feeling. He wondered if the Lucky Nugget had any private rooms, where a man could do some drinking in peace.

Before he could ask Hoagland about it, an angry voice came from down the bar, and the sound was different enough to make it instantly stand out from the loud but generally good-natured noise in the room. "Goddammit, I told you," the voice said, "one drink on the house and then you get the hell out! That's how we deal with your kind here."

Fury had turned his head when the yelling started, and he saw that the words were coming from the bullet-headed bartender. The man had his palms flat on the bar and was leaning forward in a belligerent posture as he glared at someone standing in front of him. Fury couldn't see who that was, because there were too many other people between him and that spot along the bar.

Inclining his head toward the commotion, Fury asked Hoagland, "What's that all about?"

"Nothing for you to worry about, friend," Hoagland said. "Mickey'll handle it."

Evidently Mickey was the burly bartender. Whoever he was bracing must have made an equally angry reply, because Mickey suddenly reached under the bar and brought out a bungstarter. Brandishing the club, he howled, "You can't talk to me like that, you bastard!"

The other noises in the saloon had started fading away at the first sound of trouble, but now they all died abruptly. The crowd around Fury began thinning quickly as folks ducked back away from the anticipated violence. Suddenly, through the crowd, Fury caught his first glimpse of the man who was stubbornly confronting Mickey.

Fury moved.

He didn't stop to think about it. The whole thing was instinctive. One minute he was watching the goings-on curiously, the next he was bulling forward. Behind the mahogany, the bartender called Mickey whipped the bungstarter toward his opponent's head.

Fury's hand shot forward, his fingers wrapping around Mickey's thick wrist and stopping the blow in midair. The muscles of his arm and shoulder shivered a little from the effort.

"That's enough," he said quietly.

Mickey gasped in surprise, and he wasn't the only one. Most of the bystanders who had formed a circle around the action were just as surprised.

"Fury!" the young man who was the object of the bartender's wrath exclaimed.

"Hello, Joe," Fury replied without taking his eyes off of Mickey.

Enraged at being stopped, Mickey demanded, "Is this nigger a friend of yours, mister?"

"He's a free man," Fury snapped back. "And the best damned wagon train guide this side of the Mississippi. *And* he's more than fitting to have a drink in a place like this. Now how about putting down that bungstarter and pouring my friend another drink?"

Mickey grimaced. "Well, if you put it that way . . ." He relaxed, and when Fury released his wrist, he began to lower the bungstarter.

At the same moment, Hoagland came hurrying down the bar, shaking his head. "No, Mickey!" he cried out.

"Watch it, Fury!" the young black man warned.

Mickey's other hand came up from behind the bar holding a Wells, Fargo scattergun with the barrels and stock both sawed off. The bartender had one of the hammers drawn back already and was reaching for the other one when Fury's hand darted out and grabbed hold of the bungstarter. He brought the club up underneath the short barrels of the shotgun, hoping he could divert Mickey's aim enough.

Otherwise, Fury was going to get his head blown clean off.

The right-hand barrel of the scattergun let go with a roar, but the muzzle was already tipped up and the charge of buckshot slammed into the ceiling. Mickey didn't have a chance to finish cocking the other barrel, because Fury ripped the bungstarter away from him, deftly reversed it, and slammed it against the side of his head. Mickey's eyes rolled up in their sockets, and he went down like his legs had suddenly turned to sand.

The other two bartenders were running to join the fracas. Not having had a clear view of what was going on, all they saw was Fury clouting their fellow drink juggler. Hoagland tried to motion them back, but they ignored him. One of the bartenders, a broad-shouldered youngster who had probably given up the gold fields for steadier employment, vaulted lithely onto the bar and then launched himself in a dive toward Fury.

Fury tried to twist out of the way, but he wasn't quite fast enough. The bartender tackled him around the shoulders, and both men went down hard on the sawdust-littered plank floor of the saloon. Joe tried to leap forward to help Fury, but a couple of men grabbed him from behind.

"We've got the nigger, Carl!" one of them called to the other bartender.

Carl climbed over the bar, not quite as athletically as the one who was now rolling around on the floor with Fury and swinging wild punches at him, but quickly enough. Obviously, the proprietor of the Lucky Nugget had chosen his bartenders partially for their strength, with the obvious exception of Hoagland, because Carl was also wide through the shoulders and heavily muscled. Setting his feet, he hooked a punch into the belly of the struggling Joe, then another and another. Joe would have doubled over gasping for air if the men on each side of him hadn't been holding him up.

Fury had wound up on the bottom, with the big young bartender on top of him, but he managed to get a hand on the man's throat and closed it tightly. The bartender's face turned a bright red as Fury cut off his air. With a heave of his body, Fury threw his opponent off, and as they rolled over, changing places, Fury slammed the young man's head against the floor a couple of times. That made the bartender go limp.

As Fury surged to his feet, he saw the beating that Joe was getting from Carl. With an angry shout, Fury leaped toward Carl's back, but he didn't get there. A leg came thrusting out from the crowd that pressed in around the battle, and Fury tripped over it. He felt his balance going and went down in a tumbling fall.

Kicks thudded into him as he tried to get back up. They drove him down again. The patrons of the Lucky Nugget had seemed friendly enough, but a crowd could turn ugly in a hurry, and that was just what this one was doing.

Fury reached out, grabbed a foot, twisted as hard as he could. The man went down, and as he fell, he cleared a little space around him. That gave Fury a chance to come up on one knee. He drove an elbow out to the side, right into the groin of another man who was reaching for him. The man staggered back, clutching at himself and howling in pain.

Fury got to his feet then and started slugging around him, clearing a path to Joe. When he found himself directly behind Carl, who was still smashing punches into the midsection of the young black man, Fury laced his fingers together and clubbed both hands into the back of Carl's neck, knocking him forward. The bartender stumbled into Joe and the men holding him, and all of them fell in a tangle of arms and legs.

Seeing a black hand sticking up from the pile of bodies, Fury grabbed it and hauled Joe free. There was no time to say anything to each other. With their chests heaving as they gasped for air, they put their backs together and turned to meet the next attack.

It seemed like everyone in the place wanted in on the brawl, and with the exception of Hoagland, who stood behind the bar wearing a lugubrious expression and shaking his head, they were all on the opposite side from Fury and Joe. Against half a dozen men or less, the two of them would have been able to hold their own.

They had no chance against forty or fifty.

Fury didn't know how long it took—probably no more than a few minutes—but he and Joe stood there back-to-back for what seemed like an hour, taking punches and slugging back at their opponents. Fury never gave a thought to reaching for the gun on his hip, or the Bowie knife, either, not even when his mouth was filled with blood and his eyes were so swollen that he could barely see who he was hitting. This was a matter to be settled with fists, and Joe felt the same way.

Eventually, though, timing betrayed them. A hard fist caught Fury in the jaw, driving his head back. The same thing happened at that moment to Joe, and the back of Fury's head cracked sharply against the back of Joe's. Bright red rockets sizzled through Fury's skull, standing out in vivid contrast to the darkness closing in around him. At least that was what it looked like. His arms and legs wouldn't do what he told them to anymore, and he felt himself sagging toward the floor.

Fury didn't completely lose consciousness. He could feel the hands grabbing him roughly and dragging him toward the door. He heard the batwing doors being slapped back and then smelled the clean night air as they emerged from the saloon. And he heard a voice he recognized as Mickey's saying, "Throw them out in the street, goddammit! I don't care if a wagon or two runs over them! Good riddance to the nigger and his friend both!"

If Fury had had a little more of his wits about him, he might have tried to catch himself. But as it was, all he could do was sail through the air and come down with a bone-jarring impact on the hard-packed dirt of the street. Joe thudded down beside him, tossed off the porch of the Lucky Nugget just like Fury. He let out a groan.

Fury rolled over. There wasn't a muscle in his body that didn't hurt, but he knew he had to keep moving or he'd pass out. If he lost consciousness, a wagon just might roll over him in the street. Portsmouth Square was a busy place. Pushing himself first to his hands and knees, Fury staggered up onto his feet.

Nearby, Joe was trying to get up, too. Fury leaned over, steeling himself against the dizziness that threatened to engulf him, and grasped his friend's arm. "Come on," Fury muttered through swollen lips. "Got to . . . get out of here. . . ."

Laughter came from the porch of the saloon, where most of the customers and three of the four bartenders had come out to watch the fun. Only Hoagland had stayed behind the bar. Mickey, who had recovered from the blow that had knocked him out, held both Fury's black hat and Joe's battered brown one. He tossed both hats into a puddle of mud and laughed heartily, then winced a little at the pain from the bruised lump rising on his head.

"There you go, boys," he called to Fury and Joe. "Don't forget your hats."

Another man had Fury's carbine and saddlebags. He threw them into the street as well and said, "Don't get any ideas, mister. We unloaded that rifle."

Swaying a little, Fury glared at the men and said, "If I'd wanted gunplay, there'd have been powder burned before now." Trying to muster up what dignity he could, he bent and picked up his gear, then retrieved Joe's hat as well and offered it to the young black man.

Joe took it, scowled at Mickey, and said, "You're one lucky son of a bitch. This is John Fury." Obviously, he expected the bartender to recognize the name.

"That don't mean shit to me, boy. Now get out of here, 'fore you get a worse beating."

Joe's right hand made a slight move toward the revolver holstered on his hip, but Fury reached out to stop him. The world had stopped spinning so crazily now, or at least slowed down a little, and Fury was thinking straight again. "It's not worth getting strung up by a vigilance committee, Joe," he warned in a low voice.

For a few seconds, Joe still stood there stiffly, then he took a deep breath and relaxed a little. "Yeah, you're right," he said. He looked over at Fury. "You got a place to stay?"

"Not yet."

"Well, I do. Let's find a saloon where they're willing to sell us a bottle, and then we'll go have a drink in peace."

"Sounds like a good idea to me," Fury said. Side by side, still moving gingerly, the two old friends moved away down the street, Fury untying his dun and the mule and leading them along behind. The customers from the Lucky Nugget jeered a little as the two men left, then they went back inside to resume their own celebrating.

Mickey went behind the bar again and glowered at Hoagland, who was perched on a stool waiting for the drinkers to return. The bullet-headed bartender growled, "Who the hell's John Fury, anyway?"

"Remember that Texan who was in here about two weeks ago, talking about a man who faced down a whole gang of outlaws in San Antonio a few years back and shot it out with all of them? Downed every one of the bandits even though they put two bullets in him?"

"Yeah, I remember." Mickey shook his head. "Figured that damned Texas boy was making it all up."

"Nope. It happened. I was there, and I saw the fella who did it. Saw him again tonight, too, though I could tell he didn't remember me at all."

"You mean . . ."

"That was John Fury," Hoagland said.

Mickey swallowed hard, the color washing out of his face, and turned toward the bottles arrayed behind the bar.

"I got to get me a drink," he said.

CHAPTER
4
....

Fury was surprised when Joe led him to a respectable-looking rooming house at the foot of Russian Hill. Not that Joe deserved any less than a decent place to stay because of his color; it was just that Fury hadn't found too many people who shared that attitude. He had run into plenty of folks who said that slavery was wrong and ought to be done away with, but when they owned hotels or saloons or restaurants, they were usually pretty slow to practice what they preached.

"An Italian lady owns the place," Joe explained as he showed Fury the small stable in the rear and they put away the horses. "She's a widow woman, needs the money her boarders bring in ever since her husband got killed up at a mining claim last year. She doesn't seem to mind renting a room to a colored man."

"You been in these parts long?" Fury asked.

Joe shook his head. "Nope." A grin split his young face. "Came to find me some gold and get rich."

"What happened to working as a scout for the wagon trains coming west?"

"That was fine for a while," Joe said. "But when a man gets older, he starts to think about settling down."

Fury grinned back at him as they went in the rear door of the boarding house. "Just how old *are* you? Twenty-one, twenty-two?"

"Be twenty-two in June," Joe replied.

"Yep, you're getting some years on you, all right," Fury said dryly.

There was still a light in the parlor of the house, although it appeared that most of the boarders had already gone to bed. A tall, slender woman with dark hair shot through with gray appeared in the parlor doorway as Joe and Fury entered the hall and headed for the stairs. She said sternly, "There you are, Mr. Brackett. You missed supper, you know."

"Ah, yes, ma'am," Joe said. "And I'm sorry about that."

The woman stepped closer, and a gasp escaped from her lips as she saw the bruised, battered faces of her boarder and his friend. There were still streaks of dried blood on both of their faces. "My goodness!" the woman exclaimed. "You've been in a fight."

"Yes, ma'am. But it's nothing for you to worry over. We'll be fine."

Crossing her arms across her chest, the woman looked at them sternly and said, "I don't like troublemakers in my house, Mr. Brackett. I thought I made that abundantly clear."

"Oh, you did, ma'am."

Fury tugged his hat off and put in, "The fight wasn't Joe's fault, ma'am. It was a bullheaded bartender who started the trouble. And I don't reckon I helped matters by jumping in when I did, either."

She fixed her gaze on Fury and asked, "And who might you be, sir?"

Joe performed the introductions. "His name's John Fury. An old friend of mine from the wagon train days. Fury, this is Miz Rachel Angelisi."

"Pleased to meet you, ma'am," Fury said with a nod. When Joe had said that the boardinghouse was run by an Italian widow woman, Fury hadn't figured she would turn out to be as attractive as Rachel Angelisi, who was a damned handsome woman as far as he was concerned.

"Mr. Fury," she said in response, her voice still faintly cool. She turned her attention back to Joe and went on. "Do either of you men require medical attention?"

"No, ma'am," Joe assured her. "We'll be just fine."

"Well, then . . . there's a pot of chicken and dumplings staying warm on the stove for you, left over from supper. I think there's enough for your friend Mr. Fury, as well."

"That's mighty nice of you, Miz Angelisi, but—"

"I'll brook no arguments, Mr. Brackett. Both of you look like you could use a good meal. And there's still some coffee, too."

That made up Joe's mind. He grinned and said, "Miz Angelisi makes the best coffee in California, John. We might as well have some."

"Sounds good to me," Fury said.

Rachel Angelisi led them into a spacious dining room furnished with a long table covered with a spotless white cloth. As she went off to the kitchen to fetch the food and coffee, Fury sat down across from Joe and said, "It's been a long time."

"Yeah, it has. What have you been doing, Fury?"

His shoulders lifting in a shrug, Fury smiled slightly and said, "Some of this and some of that."

"Yeah, me too."

Joe hadn't changed much since the last time the two of them had been together, Fury thought. He was still the same brash, hot-tempered young man who had helped Fury guide a wagon train full of immigrants across the plains to Colorado Territory. Fury had gotten roped in on the journey by a promise he'd made to the original wagon master, who had died in an accident not far out of Independence, Missouri. Joe Brackett had been the chief scout on that trip, as he had been on several others, and there had been some friction at first between the two men. By the end of the journey, however, they had become good friends, allies bound together by dozens of shared dangers. The trip had seen them fighting side by side against gunmen, outlaws, savage Indians, and bad weather. For a while, after the immigrants had gotten settled in their new town, Fury and Joe had ridden together, but they were both naturally fiddle-footed, and eventually they had gone their separate ways.

Now Joe was talking about making his fortune and settling down. It was an admirable dream, Fury thought, but he figured that was all it was—a dream.

Rachel brought cups and filled them with steaming coffee, and Fury had to admit the rich aroma was appealing. The strong brew tasted just as good as it smelled. After that, Rachel carried in plates heaped with chicken and dumplings and biscuits, and both men did justice to the meal, wincing at the pain from their bruised lips as they ate but unwilling to pass up such good food just because of a little discomfort. When they had eaten their fill, Rachel refilled their cups from the coffeepot, then brought a decanter of brandy from a sideboard. She laced their coffee with it and said, "If you gentlemen don't need anything else, I believe I'll retire for the evening."

"No, ma'am, we're fine," Joe told her, and Fury echoed the sentiment.

She looked at Fury. "I assume you'll be staying with us, Mr. Fury?"

"I just got into town tonight, haven't had time to find a hotel room yet," Fury said. "If you've got room for me, I'd appreciate the place to stay."

"As it happens, I *do* have an empty room. It's two doors down from Mr. Brackett's. He can show you where it is. The room is a dollar per night."

"With meals like this, that price is more'n reasonable," Fury said with a grin. He fished a dollar out of his pocket and handed the coin to her.

"Good night, gentlemen," Rachel said as she withdrew from the dining room.

Fury waited until he heard her footsteps ascending the staircase in the center of the house before he said, "That is one impressive lady."

Joe nodded. "She surely is. Never even blinked when I asked her if she had an empty room for me." The young man grinned at Fury. "Looked like she had her eye on you, too, John. Could be she's tired of being a widow. She could use a man to help her run this place, and you're getting old enough you ought to start thinking about settling down, too."

"Not damned likely," Fury grunted. He leaned back in his chair and went on. "Now tell me about how you're going to get rich."

Joe's grin widened. "Got me a claim up in the mountains," he said. "It's going to pay off big."

"Know this for a fact, do you?"

"Pretty sure." Joe nodded. "I was riding through there and spotted a gleam on a cliff face, right above where this underground stream comes out. Got my knife and chipped open some of that rock, and there was gold in it, right enough. Then I took a pan from my pack and washed some of the dirt from the streambed. There was color in it, plenty of color." Joe's voice rose a little in his excitement. "Think about it, John. There's the vein in the cliff *plus* the dust that can be taken out of the creek. It's a payoff either way."

"Sounds like a good spot," Fury admitted. "And you claimed on it?"

"Right away. Put my markers up and lit a shuck for town. I was scared somebody was going to beat me to it, but when I got here and recorded the claim, nobody else had title to that piece of ground. It's mine, all right. Now all I've got to do is go back up there and reap the rewards."

"Got enough money to outfit yourself? Mining can be an expensive business."

Joe's enthusiastic smile waned a little. "Yeah, I know. That's the problem. By the time I got here and paid my filing fee on the claim, my poke was just about empty." He leaned forward and clasped his hands together on the table. "But I've solved that problem."

Fury wondered if Joe was expecting *him* to provide a grubstake, but before he could ask the question, Joe went on. "One of the storekeepers here in San Francisco, name of J. D. McKavett, has agreed to back me. I get all the supplies I need in exchange for a share of the profits from the claim."

That was the standard agreement, Fury knew, and he was glad Joe had already found someone to provide financial backing. Joe was a good hand to ride the trails with, and there was nobody else Fury would rather have siding him in case of real trouble, but he wasn't sure about going into business with the former scout. He was just as glad he wouldn't have to make that decision.

"Well, I wish you all the luck in the world," Fury told him. "Mining for gold's a risky venture, but it can pay off mighty handsome."

"It's going to this time," Joe said as his jaunty grin returned. He became more solemn as he went on. "There's just one thing I'm worried about . . ."

After a minute, when Joe didn't go on, Fury growled, "What's that?"

"Fella at the claims office said that folks are having a lot of trouble with claim jumpers. Everything I've heard around town since then agrees with him. In fact, I noticed some rough-looking characters trailing me down from the mountains. When I spotted them, I shook 'em off as fast as I could. I got to worrying that they saw what a good claim I found and were planning to bushwhack me so that they could come file on the place themselves. If that's what they were after, it didn't work. And I beat 'em here, too, because nobody filed on the claim before me."

"Seen any of these same gents around town?" Fury asked, wondering if Joe's theory might be right.

Joe shook his head and replied, "No, but that doesn't mean anything. There are so many people here in San Francisco that they could be here and I'd never see them. They might even have been keeping an eye on me."

Fury rasped a thumbnail over the beard stubble on his jawline and frowned in thought. After a moment, he said, "I wouldn't wander into any dark alleys, if I was you. And I'd watch my back, too."

"Figured that would be a good job for you."

The casual statement took Fury by surprise. "You did, did you? You just assumed I'd go back up to the mountains with you?"

Joe shrugged. "The idea *did* occur to me. About five seconds after I saw you jump into that fracas in the Lucky Nugget, in fact. There just wasn't any time to bring it up before everybody in there started throwing punches at us."

"What were you doing in there in the first place?" Fury wanted to know. "If you're worried that somebody might be gunning for you, it's not very smart to go wandering into a strange saloon."

"I wanted a drink. Besides, that's why I need you to throw in with me, John—to keep me out of trouble like that."

The wheels of Fury's brain were clicking over. Joe's suggestion that he join in the mining venture was the second business proposition Fury had gotten tonight. Alexander Todd had also offered him a job carrying mail up to the gold fields, and Todd had said that he would pay well for such a chore. Maybe Fury could combine the two opportunities.

Besides, if somebody was really after Joe, the young man could use somebody to sort of look after him. Joe Brackett was good with a gun, and he could handle himself in a fistfight despite his slender, wiry build. But if there was a gang of claim jumpers after the land Joe had filed on, the odds would be against him.

As if sensing Fury's indecision, Joe went on. "I'll be taking a wagonload of supplies from McKavett's store up to the claim. At least come along with me and help me guard the provisions, John. More than one wagon full of supplies has been jumped up there in that wild country."

"All right," Fury said. "I suppose I can do that. And after we get there . . . well, we'll see what happens then. I may have to make a few stops along the way, though." Quickly, he explained the proposal that Alexander Todd had made to him.

"Sounds fine to me," Joe said when Fury was finished. He held out his hand across the table. "I reckon we've got a deal."

Fury's hand clasped Joe's firmly. "A deal," he agreed.

CHAPTER
5

....

Joe was not planning on returning to the claim in the Sierra Nevada Mountains for a couple of days, which was all right with Fury. That gave him a chance to pay another visit to Alexander Todd and accept the offer of employment that the owner of the express company had made to him.

"Excellent!" Todd said when he heard the news. He reached across his desk and shook Fury's hand. "I'm glad to have you with us, Mr. Fury. I've done a bit of checking around and discovered that you're rather well-known."

"Don't believe all the stories you hear," Fury said short-ly.

Todd chuckled. "I don't. But I heard enough to be certain that you're a competent man, and that you keep your word. Trustworthiness is very important in this business, you know. When I was just starting out, after I had realized that I wasn't going to make a fortune as a miner myself, some businessmen up in Stockton asked me to deliver a shipment of gold dust for them. There was a hundred and fifty thousand dollars worth of dust in that shipment, Mr. Fury, and those men turned it over to me, a relative stranger . . . because they trusted me. And I trust you."

"I won't let you down," Fury said. "Can't say how long I'll keep the job, though. I've got a friend who has a claim up there in the gold fields. He figures he might have some trouble with claim jumpers, so I may have to stay around and help him out."

"Just let me know what your intentions are," Todd said, nodding. "I'm sure we can work something out. Now, how soon can you be ready to leave?"

"Day after tomorrow, first thing in the morning," Fury said, remembering what Joe had told him about when the supplies from McKavett's store would be ready.

"That's fine. If you'll come by here tomorrow afternoon, I'll give you the mail pouches with the deliveries you'll need to make. How familiar are you with the gold fields and the surrounding territory?"

"It's been a while since I've been through most of those parts," Fury admitted. "And I reckon things've changed some in the meantime."

"Indeed. Well, I'll give you a map and directions on how to find the places you'll need to locate. I'm sure you'll do just fine."

Fury bid farewell to Todd and went back to Rachel Angelisi's boardinghouse. Even though he had never liked staying in one place for too long, he was not going to complain about the delay in leaving San Francisco. Not when he had Rachel's superb cooking and her pleasant company to enjoy. . . .

The time passed quickly, as Fury had figured it would, and after an excellent supper the next evening, Joe said, "I'm going over to the store and make sure those supplies are loaded on the wagon like they're supposed to be. I plan to leave tomorrow morning at first light. Want to come along tonight, John?"

Fury was standing in the doorway between the hall and the parlor, one shoulder propped casually against the door frame. Some of the boarders had gone out for the evening, and the others had already headed upstairs to their rooms. Rachel was sitting in the parlor alone, ensconced in an armchair as she did some needlework. Fury glanced over his shoulder at her, then looked at Joe and shook his head.

"Reckon I'll stay here tonight," he said. "Can I trust you to stay out of trouble?"

Joe grinned at him. "I could ask you the same thing."

"Go ahead and check on your supplies," Fury said in a mock growl.

Joe reached for his hat on the hall coat tree beside the front door, and he was still grinning as he settled it on his head and left the boardinghouse. Fury waited until the door had closed behind the young man, reflecting that Joe had indeed taken pains to stay out of trouble the past couple of days. Fury figured he would continue to do so on this last night before leaving San Francisco.

Then he put Joe Brackett out of his thoughts and turned his attention to the lady in the parlor. Rachel looked lovely in a dark green, long-sleeved dress that buttoned up to her throat and had a ruff of fine lace around the neck. Fury strolled into the parlor, gestured at the sofa opposite her armchair, and asked, "Mind if I sit down?"

"Help yourself, Mr. Fury," she murmured, not looking up from the fine needlework in her hands.

Fury sank onto the cushions of the sofa, leaning back against them and heaving a sigh of pure contentment. Sitting down in a fine parlor with a pretty lady was an unusual thing for a drifter like him to be doing, but he was enjoying himself and intended to keep on doing so. His guns and his knife were upstairs in his room, because for once he didn't have to worry about being jumped by thieves who wanted his outfit or Indians who wanted his hair. It was a good feeling.

Rachel went on. "You may smoke a pipe if you wish. My late husband smoked a pipe."

"Thanks, but I don't smoke," Fury said, "except under certain circumstances. There was the time Joe and I smoked a peace pipe with a band of Cheyenne. We helped a chief called Alights on the Cloud recover a medicine arrow that a bunch of Pawnees had stolen from his people."

That made Rachel look up at him curiously. "My, you *have* had quite an adventurous life, haven't you? Joe said you knew Kit Carson and Jim Bridger and some of the other famous hunters and trappers."

"Rode the trails with many of 'em." Fury nodded. "Things were a mite different then, though. The West wasn't as settled as it is now. I reckon that sort of life's just about gone."

"You sound rather regretful."

Fury shrugged. "It was a mighty hard, lonely life sometimes, but it had its rewards, too. And I'm not talking about the money a man could make from beaver pelts."

"I know that," Rachel said softly.

Talking about the old days made Fury uncomfortable. To change the subject, he asked, "What did your husband do before the two of you came out here?"

"He was a baker," Rachel replied, a faint smile of recollection touching her lips. "He made the best bread you ever tasted, and the smell of it baking was almost as wonderful. We ran a bakery together in Boston."

"I reckon that's how those biscuits of yours came to be so good."

"Yes, I suppose."

Fury looked over at her and saw to his surprise that her eyes were shining with moisture. Was she crying? Then he realized that in an effort to turn the talk away from *his* memories, he had forced her to dredge up some of *hers*.

Feeling awkward, he leaned forward and clasped his hands together. "Sorry," he said. "Didn't mean to make you feel bad by asking questions about your husband."

Rachel shook her head and smiled. "No, that's all right. I like to remember our life together. It doesn't make me sad anymore. But I do miss him sometimes. . . ."

"I'm sure you do."

Rachel laid her needlework aside and lifted her head. "Mr. Fury," she said, "would you think it was terribly bold of me if I came over there and sat beside you for a moment?"

"No, ma'am," Fury said quietly. "Not at all."

Rachel stood up and came across the few feet of space between them, and as she sat down next to him, Fury thought she looked truly beautiful in the soft lantern light that filled the parlor. She turned her green eyes toward him and asked,

"Do you think it would be dishonoring the memory of my late husband if I asked you to put your arms around me, Mr. Fury?"

He shook his head. "No, Rachel, I don't think so. I reckon he was a good man . . . he must have been if you loved him . . . and I don't figure he'd see anything wrong with me holding you for a while."

"Good." She snuggled against him, resting her head on his shoulder as his arm went around her. She sighed and went on, "It just feels so good to be held again. . . ."

They sat there like that for a while. Fury wasn't sure how long, because he was more concerned with the soft warmth of her there beside him, the sweet smell of her hair, the beating of her heart that he could faintly feel as she leaned against him. He had grown to like Rachel Angelisi in the short time he had known her, and he wasn't going to hurt her by rushing her into anything she didn't want to do. But if she was to lift her head about now and look up at him with those green eyes again, he was by God going to kiss her.

And that was exactly what she did.

His mouth came down on hers, and her lips tasted every bit as sweet as Fury expected them to. As he kissed her, she lifted her hand and rested it lightly on his cheek, and that simple touch sent a shiver through him. His arms tightened around her, and Rachel moaned a little, low and quiet and deep in her throat.

It took a few seconds after that for Fury to hear the bell ringing.

The discordant clanging was faint, as if it came from quite a distance, but it was harsh enough and loud enough for him to finally notice it. Although he didn't really want to, he lifted his head with a frown and asked, "What's that?"

Rachel asked, "What do you mean? I don't—" Then she broke off and her eyes widened. She exclaimed, "That's the fire bell!"

Fury stiffened. He had been in other cities where a bell was used to summon volunteers for a bucket brigade in case of a dangerous fire, and evidently San Francisco employed the same system. Although he had been thoroughly enjoying the kiss with Rachel, he said, "I reckon we'd better see what's going on."

"Yes," she agreed, looking concerned as she slipped easily out of his embrace and stood up. As she hurried toward the hall, she added, "There's no telling where the fire might be, but we can probably tell from the front porch. We have a good view of the city from here."

Fury followed her to the front door of the boardinghouse and then stepped out onto the porch behind her. Footsteps clattered down the staircase in the central hall as the other boarders who were home responded to the sound of the fire bell. Three men and two women came out onto the porch to join Fury and Rachel.

"What's happening?" one of the men asked. "That's the fire bell, isn't it?"

"That's right," Rachel said. "And there is the fire." She pointed a slender finger in the direction of the downtown area. Even though night had fallen, Fury could see the thick clouds of smoke billowing up into the sky, their undersides lit a flickering red by the flames that were their source. Fury spotted the blaze itself, dancing against the darkness of the buildings around it.

"Looks like a pretty good-sized fire," Fury said. "They'll need all the help they can get putting it out. I'll go lend a hand."

Without hesitation, two of the other men echoed Fury's statement. The third one waited only a moment before announcing that he would join the bucket brigade, too.

"I should go, too," Rachel said. "Just let me get my shawl—"

Fury put his hands on her shoulders to stop her. "No need for that," he said firmly. "If you want to do something to help, start making some sandwiches for the men in the bucket brigade. They're liable to be hungry when they finally get that blaze put out."

"But I can help pass buckets," she protested.

"Wait until the fire's out before you come over there," Fury said with a shake of his head. He grinned at her. "Don't want anything to happen to my landlady. Not when she sets the best table in all of California."

"Oh, all right," Rachel agreed with a sigh. "But I don't like it."

Fury wasn't asking her to like the decision, or even to think that it was the best one. But he didn't want to be worrying about her, either, while he was trying to help bring the raging fire under control.

It seemed like half the sky was lit up by the fire as Fury and the other men hurried through the streets. Even though they were not sure which building was burning, it wasn't difficult to locate the blaze. Not with flames leaping high above the surrounding rooftops now.

Fury and his companions quickly covered the six blocks between the boardinghouse and the site of the fire. The dirt streets were thronged with people running toward the conflagration and a few running away from it. The same pioneer spirit that had led folks to settle here prompted most of them to pitch in and help during times of emergency, and this certainly qualified.

When Fury got close enough, he could see that the blaze was located in a big, single-story building that took up an entire city block by itself. That was probably lucky, because the surrounding streets would help contain the fire. Also luckily, the wind from the bay was not blowing in strongly tonight, making it more difficult for the flames to leap the open spaces around them.

Unfortunately, neither of those things helped the building that was actually on fire. It was engulfed in flames that seemed to have spread from one end of the building to the other.

A long line of men had already formed to bring water from a nearby well. Buckets were filled at the well and then passed along the line until they reached a spot close enough for men to dash forward in the face of the awful heat and hurl the water onto the flames. Even as he saw the gallant, desperate effort, Fury knew it was going to be too little too late. They were not going to be able to save the building.

But the fire had to be put out anyway, to make sure that it didn't spread to the neighboring buildings. If the blaze was not stopped, and stopped *here*, it could roll over the city like a wave, and once it was out of control, it could easily burn San Francisco to the ground. Fury had seen it happen before in other towns.

There were already enough men to pass the buckets back and forth. Fury sprinted toward the head of the line. That was where the fire would take its heaviest toll on the men battling it. The heat was worse there than anywhere else, as the men ran dangerously close to the flames to throw water on them.

One of the men trying to douse the inferno was a slender young man whose dark face was shining with sweat. Fury recognized Joe Brackett, and he thought that Joe was flinging water toward the flames with a particularly frantic intensity. Joe was practically throwing the empty buckets at the men whose job it was to pass them back to the well, then grabbing a fresh pail of water and running toward the burning building once again.

Fury's eyes were already stinging from the smoke and his nose was burning from the fiery stench in the air when he ran up to Joe and grabbed the young man's arm. "Get back away from here and get some fresh air!" Fury shouted over the crackling roar of the flames. "I'll take your place!"

"Can't!" Joe cried, tugging free from Fury's grip. "That's McKavett's store!"

The words hit Fury like a fist. It was true that he didn't have any real stake in Joe's mining claim up in the mountains—other than the fact that Joe was his friend and Fury wanted him to succeed. That was enough for a man like Fury. If the supplies Joe was supposed to take to the gold fields were going up in smoke, Joe's hopes were likely going up with them.

Fury didn't waste time arguing with Joe. Instead, he turned to take a bucket of water from one of the volunteers at the head of the line. He hesitated for an instant, receiving another surprise as he saw who was about to hand him the bucket.

A woman about thirty years old stood there, her face grimy from the smoke and her fair hair tangled. Still, she was attractive in a dark blue dress that was smudged and disheveled at the moment. From the looks of her, she had been fighting this fire for quite a while, maybe even since it had broken out. She thrust the bucket of water at Fury and snapped, "Don't stand there gawking, dammit! Go throw that on the fire!"

Fury took hold of the bucket, then wheeled and ran toward the burning building, holding the bucket as level as he could so that most of the water wouldn't slosh out. The heat pounded against him like a gigantic fist trying to hold him back. Every breath he took sent smoke and searing heat into his lungs. Fighting off a spasm of coughing that shook him, Fury darted as close to the flames as he dared and then slung the contents of the bucket into the fire.

There was an old saying in Texas, a compliment about a man being brave enough to charge Hell with a bucket of water.

For the first time, Fury figured he knew exactly what that meant.

He spun around, feeling a tiny bit of blessed relief once the waves of heat were not beating directly into his face, and ran back to a man waiting to take the empty bucket. The bucket started off on its blocks-long journey that would see it returned filled with water again. As Fury grabbed a full bucket from another volunteer, he saw Joe taking a bucket from the blond woman. From the fierce expression on her face, she wanted to charge the flames herself.

Fury wondered who she was, but there was no time to ponder the question. He ran back toward the fire and emptied his bucket, then returned to the head of the line to get another one. This time it was the woman who handed it to him again, but they didn't exchange any words.

For a long time, the flames jumped and crackled and roared as they swallowed the building, and glowing sparks rose high in the sky before winking out. With luck, none of those sparks would fall back to earth and start a fire somewhere else. Finally, the wind picked up, which was a mixed blessing because it also carried a damp mist with it. The sparks were flung farther, but they were also snuffed out more easily by the moisture in the air. The mist also made the fire inside the building begin to die down a little.

The blaze was so hot that it would have taken a hard rain to extinguish it right away, however, so the men who had answered the call of the bell had to keep battling the fire for a while longer. Sometime around midnight, the final flurry of flames was dashed into oblivion by water slung from the buckets of Fury, Joe, and several other men. The fire fighters stood there for a moment, shoulders slumped in exhaustion, buckets dangling loosely from their hands, and stared at the huge heap of charred rubble that before tonight had been McKavett's store.

Fury put his free hand on his young friend's shoulder. "I'm sorry, Joe," he muttered. "I know you were counting on those supplies."

Joe lifted an arm and wiped the sleeve across his wet, sooty face, then shook his head. "The fire didn't get my supplies," he said. "They were already all loaded up in the wagon, so when the fire broke out, J. D. and I grabbed it and rolled it a couple of blocks away. If nobody stole the gear since then, it's all right. But J. D.'s lost everything else!"

Saving the supplies that way had been a lucky break, thought Fury. The only bit of luck that had occurred tonight, in fact. J. D. McKavett was more than likely wiped out by this calamity.

The blond woman Fury had seen earlier stumbled up beside them, and her hands went to her face as she stared at the ruins of the store. A low, keening sound came from her for a moment, and then she gasped, "It's gone! It's all gone!"

She turned and threw herself into Joe's arms. He dropped the bucket he was holding and began awkwardly patting her on the back, trying to give her what rough comfort he could.

"Take it easy, J. D.," he said. "It'll be all right."

He didn't sound convinced of that at all, but what interested Fury was the way he had referred to the woman as J. D. Those were the initials of the storekeeper who was grubstaking him, weren't they?

Even under the tragic circumstances, there were some of the men in the crowd who cast hard looks at the sight of a black man holding a white woman, and Fury figured he'd better try to head off trouble. He touched Joe's shoulder again and asked, "What's going on here, Joe?"

Gently, Joe turned the woman away from the sight of the rubble and then said to Fury, "John, this is J. D. McKavett."

After Joe's comments, Fury had been halfway expecting that, but it still came as something of a surprise to have the suspicion confirmed. "J. D.?" he said.

The woman wiped tears away from her eyes, leaving wet streaks in the grime that coated her face, and she asked sharply, "What would you call yourself if you were in business and your name was Jocasta Drusilla?"

"Well, maybe J. D. is better," Fury admitted. "I'm John Fury, ma'am, and I'm sorry we have to meet under circumstances like these. Joe's told me a lot about you." He glanced at the young man and added pointedly, "Although obviously not everything."

Joe just shrugged and made no reply.

Fury asked, "What do you think caused the fire to break out?"

"Not *what*," J. D. McKavett said bitterly. "*Who*."

Fury frowned. "I don't understand."

"The fire was set," Joe replied. "I had just finished putting the last of my supplies on the wagon, and J. D. and I were standing on the porch talking when the flames started in the back of the store. It was almost like an explosion back there.

I reckon they snuck in, splashed some coal oil around, and tossed a light on it."

"They?" Fury repeated. "Who're you talking about?"

"The Hellhounds," J. D. said. "It had to be them."

Fury shook his head and said, "I've heard of the Hounds, but not the Hellhounds."

Joe's voice was grim as he said, "I told you I thought somebody tried to follow me into town, John. When I explained about that to J. D., she said it was probably the Hellhounds. They're the gang behind most of the claim jumping up in the gold fields."

J. D. explained. "When the Hounds and the Sydney Ducks were run out of San Francisco by the vigilance committees, the survivors from both gangs got together and formed a new gang. They call themselves the Hellhounds now. Joe didn't know about them until he got to town, because he hadn't been through this area before."

"They're liable to be camped out on my claim when I get back up there," Joe said. "They may even be working it already. But that'll change." His tone was hard and dangerous as he made the vow.

J. D. took a deep breath and went on. "I think the men who trailed Joe into town have been watching him and found out somehow that I was grubstaking him. They burned my store down to discourage him from returning to the gold fields and taking over his claim."

"That's a pretty vicious thing to do," Fury said, feeling anger growing inside him at what he had heard.

"It's the way that the Hellhounds operate, though," J. D. said. "They're so ruthless that most people are too afraid of them to oppose them. They're going to be surprised this time, however."

"Damn right," Joe declared. "Since we were able to save the supplies, I'm going back up to the mountains to get what's rightfully mine, and yours, too, J. D. John and I will take care of any of those Hellhounds who give us grief."

J. D. McKavett lifted her head and squared her shoulders. "You won't be traveling alone," she said. "I'm going, too."

Both Fury and Joe stared at her in shock. Fury found his tongue first. "What did you say?"

"That I'm going with you." J. D. looked on bleakly as men began poking through the cooling ashes of the ruins, searching for anything that could be salvaged. Considering the degree of destruction, it was unlikely that they would find anything. J. D. went on. "My business is gone. Practically everything I own was consumed in the fire—except that wagonload of supplies I was providing for you, Joe. Those supplies—and the share in the claim they represent—are all I have left." Despite everything that had happened, she managed to summon up a faint smile, and Fury thought she looked even prettier than before. "I guess you could say that I'm going along to help protect my investment."

Fury was shaking his head before she even finished. "Joe and I can do that," he said. "There's no need for you to go to the mountains. That would just cause trouble."

J. D. frowned at him. "And why is that?" she snapped.

Fury looked right back at her. "I shouldn't have to explain. There are hundreds, maybe thousands of men up there, and damned few women. Even fewer as young and pretty as—" He stopped, unwilling to finish the compliment.

With a humorless laugh, J. D. said, "I assure you, Mr. Fury, I'm not worried about a bunch of lonely miners losing their heads because of my beauty. My only concerns are the Hellhounds and protecting Joe's claim from them."

"And how are you going to do that?" Fury asked. "Can you handle a gun?"

She nodded without hesitation. "I'd be glad to demonstrate anytime you like."

Joe said slowly, "I don't much like the idea of you going along, either, J. D. Like John says, it could make for extra trouble."

"Well, Joe, I'm afraid you don't have much choice in the matter." She looked from one of them to the other, and the determination was easy to read on her face in the light of several torches that had been brought up by the crowd in order to survey the damage. "Those supplies still belong to me," J. D. continued, "and unless you want to find someone else to provide a stake for you, I'm going!"

Joe looked at Fury and shrugged his shoulders helplessly. "John?"

"Looks like the lady's got us backed into a corner," Fury said. "I reckon you're going along, all right, Miz McKavett."

For the first time since the fire had broken out, a smile appeared on the face of J. D. McKavett.

Fury added, "But that doesn't mean we have to like it. Be ready to leave first thing in the morning."

"I will be," J. D. promised.

And even though he had known her less than an hour, Fury believed her.

J. D. McKavett struck him as the kind of woman who wouldn't let anything stand in the way of something she wanted to do.

CHAPTER
6

....

J. D. McKavett was as good as her word. As the first light
of dawn was edging into San Francisco the next day, Fury
and Joe found the woman waiting in front of the small hotel
where she had taken a room for the night, just as arranged.
Her living quarters had been in the rear of the store and had
been destroyed in the blaze along with the rest of the building, so J. D. had been forced to find somewhere else to stay.
Fury had given her the money to rent the room, and although
she had disliked that as much as Fury disliked her decision
to accompany them to Joe's claim, she'd had no choice.

Joe brought the wagon to a stop in front of the hotel, haul-
ing back on the reins and calling, "Whoa!" to the four mules.
His buckskin was tied on at the back of the vehicle, which
was loaded with supplies that made a mound in the back,
rising above the side boards. A canvas tarpaulin had been
thrown over the load and tied down to protect it.

Fury was riding his dun alongside the wagon, and he was
tired. The night before, he and Joe had rolled the wagon back
to Rachel Angelisi's boardinghouse and into the small stable at the rear. Since the Hellhounds hadn't hesitated to burn
down J. D.'s store, Fury was sure they would be equally ruthless if they found out the supplies had survived the fire. He
and Joe had spent the night in the stable to keep an eye on
the provisions.

The two men had risen long before daylight. They'd picked
up the team of mules that Joe had arranged for—bought with

57

J. D. McKavett's money as part of the grubstake—and brought the animals back to Rachel's to harness them.

Rachel had a big breakfast ready: biscuits, ham and eggs, stacks of flapjacks, and plenty of hot, strong coffee. That made Fury feel a little better, but then there had been the farewell to the handsome widow, and that had depressed him once again.

Still, he could remember the way her lips had brushed against his in a quick kiss and how she had murmured, "I hope you'll come back here from the mountains sometime."

"I'll do that," Fury had said. He intended to keep that promise.

Now he and Joe were ready to pick up J. D. McKavett and head for the Sierra Nevada, and from the expectant look on her face as she greeted them, J. D. was ready, too.

"I hope the Hellhounds didn't pay you another visit last night," she said as Joe helped her up onto the wagon seat.

"Didn't see hide nor hair of them," Joe said. "No trouble at all, in fact."

"That's good." J. D. settled down on the hard wooden bench. "Perhaps our luck has changed, and we'll not see any more of them."

Fury figured she didn't believe that any more than he and Joe did, but there was no point in saying anything. He heeled the dun into motion as Joe got the wagon rolling again.

After riding in silence for a few moments, Fury said, "I've got to make a stop on the way out of town. Alexander Todd's supposed to have a bag of mail ready for me to pick up and carry to the mountains."

"You're delivering the mail, Mr. Fury?" J. D. asked. She had scrounged up another dress somewhere, this one a lighter blue, decorated with little yellow flowers. Her face had been washed and no longer bore any trace of the grime and soot of the night before. The long, flowing blond hair had been brushed until it glistened. J. D. looked younger this morning than she had the night before, hardly old enough, in fact, to have been the owner of a store.

"Carrying the mail's just a temporary job," Fury told her, then went on to explain the errand that had brought him to San Francisco in the first place, as well as the business proposition that Alexander Todd had made to him. "I figured as long as I was heading up into the mountains anyway, I might as well give Todd a hand."

"And make some money in the process," J. D. pointed out.

Fury shrugged. "That too," he admitted.

Joe stopped the wagon in front of the building where Todd's office was located, then took the dun's reins when Fury had swung down from the saddle. "I won't be in there long," Fury promised.

Todd was waiting for him, just as planned. The owner of the express company turned over two hefty canvas bags filled with mail.

"I'll take good care of 'em," Fury said. "What do I do with the dust I collect for delivering the letters?"

"Well, I hope you bring it back to me yourself and continue working for me," Todd replied. "If you decide not to do that, though, I have an agent in Sonora. You can turn the dust over to him, and he'll see that it gets back here to me. You can also give him any outgoing letters you've picked up on the way."

"Sounds good." Fury extended his hand to the expressman. "Pleasure meeting you, Mr. Todd. Hope to see you again."

"I hope so, too," Alexander Todd said.

The sun was rising higher in the sky by the time Fury rejoined his two companions, but it had not completely burned through the early morning fog just yet. Quickly, Fury rigged a rawhide thong so that it was fastened to both pouches of mail, then looped it around his saddle horn and let the bags hang off, one on each side of the horse. "Ready to go," he said as he stepped up into the saddle.

Joe flapped the reins, yelled at the team, and laid a short whip across the rumps of the mules. With a lurch and a jolt that nearly unseated J. D., the wagon got under way again.

Riding alongside the vehicle, Fury asked, "How well do you know this country, Miz McKavett?"

"Please, call me J. D.," she said. "Mrs. McKavett was my late husband's mother."

So she was a widow woman, too, thought Fury, just like Rachel Angelisi. Well, that wasn't unusual. Lots of men died out here in the West, and most of them left wives and sometimes kids behind. He wondered suddenly if J. D. had any children. Joe hadn't said anything about any youngsters—but then he hadn't told Fury that the masculinely named J. D. McKavett was a woman, either, and a damned attractive one at that.

Deciding it was too personal a question to bring up, Fury kept his mouth shut. Joe drove the wagon down to the bay, where the ferry was already operating this morning. The wagon clattered aboard the big barge, along with a couple of buggies and several men on horseback, and the long voyage across the bay began.

With the heavily loaded wagon to slow them down, it would take about a week to reach the claim, Joe said. The roads were not very good. Fury could vouch for that, having recently passed through the area himself. That first day, they didn't reach any of the gold fields where Fury would be delivering letters, but they probably would by the second day. By the light of their campfire that night, he unfolded the map Alexander Todd had given him and studied it.

Joe was frying up some bacon in a big skillet, and in another pan, beans that had been soaking all day while they traveled were now cooking. J. D. came around the fire, gestured at the paper in Fury's hand, and asked, "What's that?"

"Just a map," he told her. "Shows me where I'm supposed to drop off some of those letters I'm carrying."

"Can I see it?" She waved a hand at the fire and made a self-deprecating face. "I'd help Joe, but I'm afraid I'm not a very good cook. I can't even make coffee."

"Sure, sit down," Fury said, struck once again by both the similarities and the differences between J. D. and Rachel. Both were attractive and both were widows, but that seemed to be where the similarities ended. Rachel was dark and J. D. was fair, and while Fury figured Rachel might well be the best cook in San Francisco—maybe in all of California—J. D. made no pretense of being able to fix a decent meal.

Fury was sitting on the ground and leaning back against a fallen log. J. D. settled down on the log itself and looked over Fury's shoulder at the map.

"What names these places have," J. D. commented. "Hangtown, Buzzard Gulch, Dead Man's Sluice. . . . Who comes up with them?"

"It's violent country," Fury said with a shrug of his shoulders. "A lot of men go into the mountains looking for gold and never come back out again. That's one reason I didn't want you coming along."

J. D. sniffed, a delicate sound that somehow managed to seem as contemptuous as the snort of a mule. "I know it's dangerous. I've sold supplies to a great many of those miners, Mr. Fury. But I don't intend to sit back and see my investment in Joe's claim be stolen from me."

Joe looked up from his cooking. "We wouldn't cheat you," he said quietly.

The woman had the good grace to blush. Hurriedly, she said, "Oh, I didn't mean that, Joe, and you know it! I was talking about those awful Hellhounds."

"I know that," Joe said, grinning slyly as he turned his attention back to the bacon and beans. "Just joshin' you."

"I'm not sure the lady appreciates your sense of humor, Joe," Fury said dryly.

J. D. just glared at both of them for a moment, then stood up and went over to sit on the lowered tailgate of the wagon. "Supper'll be ready in a minute," Joe called to her.

"I'm not sure I'm hungry."

"Suit yourself."

J. D. ate when the time came, however, and seemed to get over her momentary chagrin as she enjoyed the food. It *was* good, Fury admitted to himself. Not as good as the meals that Rachel Angelisi had fed them, of course, but not bad. Joe was a better cook than Fury would have given him credit for.

"I had to learn *something* on all those wagon trains," Joe said after Fury had commented on the meal.

When they were finished eating, J. D. insisted on cleaning up after the meal, and while she was doing that, Fury and Joe checked on the horses and the mules, making sure the animals were settled for the night. There was plenty of graze here at the spot they had selected for their camp, and Fury figured they would be fine until morning.

"We'd better stand watches," Joe said in a low voice, glancing toward J. D. "She's liable to insist on taking a turn."

"She can insist all she wants to," Fury said. "Until we can be sure she'll stay awake and alert—and that she can handle a gun—I don't reckon I'd sleep any too good with her on guard."

Joe grinned. "Then *you* can tell her that."

"Be glad to," Fury grunted.

As expected, J. D. put up a little fuss when Fury explained that he and Joe would be splitting the guard shifts. But Fury didn't budge from his decision, and J. D. wound up stalking off to roll herself up in her blankets underneath the wagon. Joe took a spot near the embers of the fire, and Fury stood the first watch.

It was quiet and peaceful out there once everybody was settled down, nothing to keep a man company but the faint rustlings and scurryings of small animals in the brush and the occasional mournful hoot of an owl. Fury had no trouble staying awake, though. He'd stood many a night guard just like this. His life, and the lives of Joe and J. D., could depend on his watchfulness.

No trouble visited the camp that night, however, either during Fury's watch or Joe's during the wee hours. By sunrise the next morning, they were up and rolling again, heading deeper into the mountains.

These thickly wooded heights, with their twisting valleys in between, were well-populated now. People had been pouring into the area ever since that fateful day in '48. Fury, Joe, and J. D. saw quite a few other travelers on the road, and they passed a couple of settlements during the morning, small communities made up mostly of tents and crude log or plank huts. A few men came out to say hello and ask for news from San Francisco, and Fury saw how their eyes lit up at the sight of J. D. They were polite, though, and kept their thoughts to themselves, although Fury imagined there would be more than one desperately lonely man moaning in his sleep that night as he dreamed of the pretty blonde who had momentarily brightened his existence.

The third settlement they reached was called Callisto, and Fury had a letter in one of the pouches for a miner who lived there. He dug it out, double-checked the map to make sure he had the right place, and then went looking for one Homer Deakins.

After a couple of stops to question men wielding picks and shovels as they chipped away at a rocky hillside, Fury was directed to a shack set about a hundred yards up the steep slope. He left the dun with Joe and J. D. at the wagon and started up the hill on foot, carrying the letter in his left hand.

He was about thirty yards from the hut when a gun blasted.

In the next instant, Fury heard the bullet whip over his head, but he was already diving ahead to the ground. There was no cover here; he was a sitting duck. Twisting his head around as he drew the big Colt, he bawled to Joe and J. D., "Get behind the wagon!"

The rifle cracked again, and a bullet whined off the stony ground several yards to Fury's left. This time he saw a puff of smoke from the corner of the shack and knew the rifleman was using the flimsy structure for cover. If the range had been a little closer, Fury knew he could have punched a ball from the Dragoon right through the boards of the shack, but the big revolver wasn't built for a long-distance shoot-out.

He ducked his head as another shot erupted from the cabin and the bullet kicked up rock dust to his right.

The gunman had bracketed him, a shot above his head, one to his left, one to his right. Fury knew the message the man was sending even before the harsh voice called out, "The next one goes right through you, mister, less'n you tell me what the hell you're doin' on my claim!"

Alexander Todd might've mentioned that some of the customers were a little trigger-happy, Fury thought. He lifted his left hand, the one with the letter in it, and shouted, "I've got your mail here, you damned fool!"

There was a momentary silence from the shack, then the same voice asked, "That's a letter . . . for me?"

"Are you Homer Deakins?" Fury asked, lifting himself a little more from the ground.

"That's right." The voice hardened again. "I didn't tell you to get up, mister!"

Fury grimaced and crouched lower again. "Look," he called, "if you don't want this letter, it's all right with me."

"Hold on, hold on," Homer Deakins said impatiently. He emerged from the cabin, a tall, bearded man holding a Colt's revolving rifle aimed unerringly at Fury. "Didn't say I don't want my mail. But you ain't the feller what brung it before."

"Todd just hired me," Fury explained. "If you'll let me get up, you can take a look at this letter and see for yourself that I'm telling the truth."

"All right," Deakins growled. "But holster that hogleg first, and if I see you reachin' for it again, I'll ventilate you, sure as hell."

Fury slipped the pistol back in its holster as he rose to his feet. Keeping his hands extended slightly to the side so that Deakins could see them clearly, he walked toward the cabin. When he got closer, he saw that Deakins was barrel-chested, with a large nose and tattered overalls worn over red long johns. Deakins stuck out a callused hand and snapped, "Gimme that letter."

Fury handed it over and said, "That'll be an ounce of gold dust, just like you agreed with Todd."

"Yeah, yeah, just hold on to your britches," Deakins muttered. Holding the rifle with one hand, he used the other and his teeth to open the letter, and when he had the sheet of paper unfolded, he frowned at it as he scanned the words scrawled there.

Abruptly, Deakins looked up at Fury, and a grin broke out on his wrinkled face. "It's from my wife," he said. "I got me another young'un. A boy!"

"Congratulations," Fury said. "Now how about pointing that rifle somewhere else?"

Deakins uncocked the rifle and tucked it under his arm. "Sure, sure. Sorry 'bout shootin' at you, mister. When I seen you comin', I was afraid you was one o' them damned Hellhounds."

"Had a lot of trouble with them in these parts, eh?"

"Not me yet, thank the Lord," Deakins said emphatically. "But I know fellers who've had their claims jumped by 'em." The miner frowned darkly and shook his head. "Some o' my friends've wound up dead after standin' up to the Hellhounds."

"Sorry to hear it," Fury said. "We've got to be moving on, Deakins. I need that dust you owe Todd."

"I'll get it." Deakins looked past Fury and down the slope at Joe and J. D. "Friends o' your'n?"

"Partners, I guess you could say." That was stretching it a little, thought Fury, but what the hell.

"I'll get that dust from the shack, and I got a bottle in there, too. How about the three of you havin' a drink with me to celebrate the brand-new Deakins younker?"

"I reckon we can do that," Fury said with a smile. The miner was lonely, anxious for company and anxious to share his joy at the news of the recently arrived baby. Besides, Fury felt a little grateful to the man.

After all, Deakins hadn't shot him.

CHAPTER
7

....

If Fury had expected J. D. McKavett to be reluctant to share a drink with Deakins, then he was bound to be disappointed. Because J. D. didn't seem to mind at all. In fact, she shook hands with the man, congratulated him on his new child, and then tipped the bottle of whiskey to her mouth just like Fury, Joe, and Deakins had done before her. Then she wiped the back of her other hand across her mouth and passed the bottle back to Deakins without flinching, even though the stuff had the kick of a Missouri mule.

"I gotta say, ma'am, you ain't like any lady I ever run into before," Deakins commented. "Most of 'em wouldn't have nothin' to do with a scroungy ol' rat like me."

"Nonsense, Mr. Deakins," J. D. declared. "You seem like a fine upstanding citizen to me, and I can tell from the way you reacted to the news of your child's birth that you love your family."

"Sure do."

"I'm a businesswoman, Mr. Deakins, and I've learned it doesn't pay to prejudge people."

"What are the three of you doin' here in the mountains, anyway?" Deakins asked.

"We're going to work a gold claim," Joe said, "up at Last Chance Canyon."

Fury looked sharply at him. "You hadn't mentioned where that claim of yours is located. Last Chance Canyon, eh?"

Deakins frowned and shook his head. "Rough country up yonder, and lots of rough gents around. I hear the stronghold o' the Hellhounds ain't far from there."

"We'll deal with the Hellhounds," Joe promised.

"You be mighty careful up there," Deakins advised. "Especially you, ma'am."

"I intend to be, Mr. Deakins," J. D. assured him.

They moved on from Callisto to Bergen's Gap, to Fletcherville, to Sour Springs. Fury delivered a few letters in each place, and the small leather pouch in which he carried the gold dust he was paid began to get heavier. He had also picked up a few letters to be taken back to San Francisco and mailed, and for each of those he had collected two dollars and fifty cents.

Everyplace the travelers stopped over the next few days, they were warned about the Hellhounds. Obviously, the gang had this whole section of the Sierra Nevada worried. Fury enjoyed delivering the mail—especially since nobody had shot at him since Homer Deakins—but he had a feeling he would be giving up the job once they arrived at the claim and he had a chance to see how things were there. Fury's instincts told him Joe might need help, and a lot of it. If the situation was bad, Fury would leave just long enough to take the gold dust and the outgoing mail over to Alexander Todd's agent in Sonora.

When they were still a good two days from the claim, trouble cropped up again. The road was following a small creek that twisted and turned through the mountain valleys, and as Joe sent the wagon around a particularly sharp bend, a rifle cracked somewhere above them and to their right. Fury reined in, listening for the sound of a bullet so that he would know if the unseen gunman was shooting at them. He didn't hear anything, but then the rifle barked again, and something hummed past Fury's ear.

They were targets, all right.

Fury spurred the dun forward and yelled, "Get off the road!" to Joe, who was already whipping the team and sending the mules toward the edge of the trail. J. D. hunkered down low beside him on the seat.

Fury rode past the wagon and waved toward a small stand of pines that would give them some cover. The ground around the pines was rather bare, however, and once they had taken shelter there, the rifleman would have them pinned down. Fury didn't want that.

He heard the rifle blast a third time, saw the faint drift of gun smoke coming from a clump of rocks on the hillside. That was where the bushwhacker was hiding. Fury had just turned the dun toward the slope when the rifle spoke again.

Fury pitched loosely out of the saddle.

He hit hard, rolled over a couple of times, and dropped out of sight. Joe saw what had happened and yelled, "Fury!" He brought the wagon to a sliding stop behind the trees and hustled J. D. off the seat and behind the vehicle for the extra protection it would provide. Then he yanked his carbine from the back of the wagon and ran to the forward edge of the trees. Kneeling behind one of the pines, he brought the carbine to his shoulder and sent a shot into the rocks where the ambusher was hidden. A moment later, as he reloaded, another bullet came whipping through the trees, and Joe knew his shot hadn't done any good.

Anger burned brightly inside him. John Fury was as good a man as Joe had ever known, a man to ride the river with, and somebody had ruthlessly cut him down from ambush.

That was when Joe spotted the flicker of motion on the hillside, below and off to the right of the rocks.

Fury crouched in the shallow gully he had noticed just before the ambusher cut loose at him again. Acting almost instantaneously with the thought, Fury had flung himself out of the saddle, deliberately falling as if the shot had hit home. A couple of rolls had taken him over the lip of the gully that zigzagged up the hill.

If it was deep enough all the way up, Fury figured he could work his way past the bushwhacker and then jump the bastard from behind. It had taken him a few minutes to catch his breath, which had been knocked out of him by the fall from the horse, but then he had started moving on hands and knees up the slash in the hillside, cut there either by an earthquake or by the flow of water during the rainy times.

Fury was fairly sure he was shielded from the view of the rifleman, but he didn't know if Joe and J. D. could see him or not. Probably not, he decided, and he wished he could signal them in some way to let them know that he was actually all right. But that would mean taking a chance of exposing himself to the bushwhacker, too.

Besides, if this spur-of-the-moment plan didn't work out, he more than likely *wouldn't* be all right.

A couple of times during the ascent, the gully became so shallow that Fury had to lower himself to his belly and inch along using his elbows and toes to push himself up the slope. It was slow going, and the sound of the rifle as it kept throwing bullets toward the trees was maddening. If one of those shots struck J. D. or Joe . . . Fury had to fight off the impulse to rise to his feet and rush head-on toward the rocks.

Finally, though, he was past the spot where the ambusher was hidden. He went on another ten or fifteen feet, then slithered out of the gully, being careful not to dislodge any pebbles that could clatter down the slope and warn the attacker that someone was behind him. Then, with a whisper of steel against leather, Fury drew his Colt and began working his way toward the rocks.

Now Joe would be able to see him, and sure enough, the regularly spaced shots from the trees stopped for a moment, then resumed even faster than before. The sound of the shots might cover up any noises he would make in slipping up on the gunman, Fury hoped. Another few steps, and he ought to be able to see the man. . . .

There! Fury spotted him, crouched behind the rocks and aiming through a small gap between a couple of them. From this angle, Fury couldn't tell anything about the bushwhacker except that he was a man, dressed in dark pants and coat and wearing a hat with a wide, drooping brim. Fury edged closer.

From this vantage point, Fury could have put a ball through the man's back, but he had never been one to shoot somebody from behind, not even a low-down bushwhacker. Joe was still firing from down in the trees, his shots thudding into the hillside just below the rocks, aimed there deliberately so that he wouldn't accidentally hit Fury. With that threat to distract the ambusher, Fury took a chance and moved still closer, until he was only about ten feet up the slope from the man.

With his thumb on the hammer of the Dragoon, ready to cock it immediately if he had to, Fury set himself and waited until the ambusher had emptied the magazine tube of his Smith-Jennings repeater. Then, as the man reached into his pocket for more cartridges, Fury called out, "Drop the gun, mister!"

With a gasp, the man whirled around and started to bring up the barrel of the rifle, then realized it was empty and no good to him. Cursing, he flung the weapon at Fury and grabbed desperately under his coat for a pistol.

Fury ducked the thrown rifle and darted forward, and as the man jerked a small revolver from under his coat, Fury lashed out. The toe of his boot caught the man in the wrist, sending the pistol spinning away and clattering down the slope. The man cried out in pain and clutched his wrist. Fury cocked and leveled the Dragoon and ordered coldly, "You just stay still, boy, and don't give me any more reasons to blow your brains out."

The ambusher was a slender young man with a pale, narrow face and a shock of black hair sticking out from under the floppy-brimmed hat. He stared up at Fury, his features taut with fear and anger and pain, and he said hotly, "Go ahead and shoot me, you son of a bitch! You've already ruined my life. You might as well go ahead and kill me!"

"Ruined your life?" Fury repeated. "What in blazes are you talking about? I never saw you before now, boy."

His voice shaking with the depth of the emotion he was feeling, the young man said, "You made me lose my job. And you killed my brother!"

If the man had only accused Fury of killing his brother, Fury might have believed him. He had been in more than his share of gunfights and was still alive, which meant that most of the men he had faced had died. More than once in the past, he had found himself tracked down and braced by relatives of somebody who had drawn on him. But the business of making this youngster lose his job . . . that was what had Fury confused.

"I still don't know what you're talking about, son," Fury told him. "But get up anyway, and don't try anything. I'd hate to shoot you before I find out what's going on here, but I will if I have to."

The youngster got to his feet as Fury covered him, and when the man was standing up, Fury waved down to Joe and J. D. to let them know that everything was under control. From the corner of his eye, he saw Joe emerge from the trees and return the wave.

"Get on down the hill," Fury grunted, gesturing with the long barrel of the Dragoon.

The young man started climbing rather clumsily down the slope, his hands lifted. Fury followed behind him with the gun, close but not too close.

If this gent was one of the Hellhounds, then Fury thought the gang had been seriously overrated. Any man with a rifle in his hands could be trouble, but this gawky youngster struck Fury only as a minor threat. Any damage he did might well be accidental.

Joe pulled the wagon out of the trees as Fury approached with the prisoner, then the former scout hopped down from the seat and drew his pistol. J. D. stayed on the wagon, but she had Joe's carbine in her lap, and from her tense posture and watchful gaze, she knew what to do with it.

"Who have you got there, Fury?" Joe asked.

"A young scarecrow, from the looks of him," Fury replied. And to tell the truth, the young man with his gaunt figure and patched, ragged clothes did look something like a scarecrow. Fury went on. "He hasn't told me his name, or why he started taking potshots at us."

The young man stopped and said savagely over his shoulder, "My name's Milo Phipps. And I told you why I was shooting at you!"

"Milo Phipps!" Fury exclaimed. "You mean you're Johnny's brother?"

"That's right," Milo answered bitterly. "He *was* my brother. He's dead now, 'cause of you."

"Wait just a minute," Fury said, his tone sharp. "You're all mixed-up, kid. I didn't kill your brother. Some hard cases who wanted to loot his mail pouch did that. *They're* the ones I killed, and that's how I got the sack of mail back."

"That's your story," Milo Phipps said with a snort of disbelief. "I think you wanted the job for yourself, so you killed Johnny. You didn't even know he wasn't the regular express rider. That was *my* run!" Milo's voice threatened to break as he went on. "Poor ol' Johnny was just helping me out."

"I know," Fury told him. "Alexander Todd told me the whole story. Look, Phipps, I'm sorry about your brother. But I didn't kill him or have anything to do with his death. All I did was bury him and then later on take care of the weasels who gunned him down."

Milo still looked dubious. "You expect me to believe you?"

"Dammit, think about what you're saying," Joe said in exasperation. "If Fury was the kind of gent to do that sort of thing, do you think he'd have gone to the trouble of disarming you once he had the drop on you just now? Hell no! He'd have just put a bullet in your back and gone on about his business!"

For the first time, Milo Phipps seemed a little doubtful. He glared at Fury and asked, "You got any proof that things happened like you say they did?"

Fury pointed to the northwest and said, "Go about twelve or fourteen miles in that direction and you'll find the Narwhale Trading Post, run by a fella named Ross. He and his wife and daughter saw me trade lead with the men who killed your brother. They'll back up my story."

"I know the Rosses," Milo said with a frown. "Always figured they were honest."

"So you see, Mr. Phipps," J. D. said, "Mr. Fury is telling the truth about your brother."

"Reckon so," Milo grumbled. "Can I put my hands down now?"

"You planning on trying anything else?" Fury asked.

Milo shook his head.

"Put 'em down. Joe, why don't you get his rifle and pistol? But unload the pistol before you bring them down here."

"Sure, John," Joe said. He started up the slope to retrieve the weapons.

"Now, what's this about losing your job?" Fury asked the young man.

"Mr. Todd fired me," Milo said with a sigh. "I reckon he was mad that I let Johnny take my run without checking with him first. He said it was just pure luck I didn't cost him a bunch of money. Then he told me that he'd hired you to take my place. That didn't seem fair. The more I thought about it, the more I figured maybe you weren't telling the truth about what really happened. So I followed you when you left town, figured I'd even the score with you for Johnny."

"You know now that you were wrong, though," J. D. said. "So you don't have any reason to bother us in the future, do you?"

"No, ma'am," Milo muttered, his eyes downcast. "Don't guess I do."

Joe returned with the Smith-Jennings rifle and the pistol, a Colt pocket model. He handed them to Milo, then dropped the cartridges from the pistol in Milo's coat pocket. "Don't try loading 'em again until you've put some miles between us, mister," Joe warned.

"Don't worry, I won't make no more trouble." Milo sighed heavily again. "I suppose I'll go back to San Francisco, try to get some other sort of job there. I sure as hell ain't cut out to be a miner. Johnny and I gave that our best shot 'fore I ever went to work for Mr. Todd."

"Just stay out of trouble, son," Fury told him. "And try not to cross our path again."

Milo nodded gloomily.

"Where's your horse?"

"Back up over the ridge," Milo said, waving toward the top of the slope.

"Go get it and get the hell out of here," Fury said.

Milo did as he was told, trudging up the hill to disappear over the top of it. As the vengeful young man vanished, Joe asked, "You reckon we've seen the last of him?"

"Surely he wouldn't try to ambush us again," J. D. said. "Not now that he's been set straight."

"I wouldn't count on it," Fury said, rubbing his jaw in thought. "I reckon deep down he blames himself for his brother getting killed, since Johnny was taking his place. It's hard for folks to live with a thing like that, so sometimes they start looking around for somebody else to blame, even if it doesn't really make sense. And once they've got that notion in their heads, it's hard to let go of it."

"I wouldn't have taken you for a philosopher, Mr. Fury."

Fury looked at J. D. McKavett. "I've learned a few things over the years, like being able to look at a man and tell a little about what he's thinking and feeling. That's as much a part of staying alive as knowing how to handle a gun or a knife."

She flushed a little and turned away. "I think we should be going," she said.

As they got moving again, Fury thought about Milo Phipps. Some of Milo's shots had come pretty close, even though he hadn't put up much of a fight when Fury jumped him. Milo struck him as the sort to foul up most things he touched, but even a hard-luck case like that could sometimes get lucky enough to be dangerous. In the meantime, they still had the Hellhounds to worry about.

Yep, Fury thought, delivering the mail was turning out to be a pretty interesting job after all.

CHAPTER
8

....

Two more days of traveling brought them to Last Chance Canyon late in the afternoon. It was a deep, steep-sided valley about a half mile wide and five or six miles long. The walls were high and rugged, with a few pines dotting the rimrock on both sides. As Fury, Joe, and J. D. entered the canyon, Joe pointed out a small trickle of water that ran through its center.

"That's the stream I was telling you about," he said. "It curves back to the left about halfway up the canyon and runs over to the cliff on that side. That's where the springs come up, right there where my claim is."

Fury's keen eyes scanned as much as he could see of the canyon. "Smoke up ahead," he said. "Looks like cook fires, several of them."

"Could be," Joe said. "I didn't see anybody when I first came through here, but there could be some other claims. In fact, I'd be surprised if there wasn't."

So would Fury. It would be unusual to find any good-sized canyon here in the Sierra Nevada that didn't have some miners working to make a strike in it.

Suddenly, Joe hauled back on the reins and pulled the mules to a halt. He handed the reins to J. D. and said, "I think I'll untie that buckskin of mine and ride on ahead with John if you don't mind, J. D. You can bring the wagon on to the claim, can't you?"

"Well, I suppose," J. D. replied, looking somewhat surprised by the request, as was Fury. "I can handle a team of mules. I've done it before. But are you sure I can find the place?"

"Just follow the creek," Joe told her. "You can't miss it." He hopped down lithely from the seat and went to the back of the wagon to untie his saddle horse.

Fury wondered just why Joe was doing this, and at the same time he felt a little uneasy about leaving J. D. alone with the wagon. What if she ran into trouble while she was bringing it on to the claim? But Fury knew Joe well enough to be sure that the former scout would not have made the suggestion without a good reason. He didn't say anything, just sat on the dun with his hands crossed and resting on the saddle horn, while Joe swung up on the buckskin.

"Ready to go?" Joe asked Fury.

"This is your bailiwick," Fury said. "Lead the way."

The two men put their horses into a trot as they left the wagon behind. Joe followed the creek, just as he had advised J. D. to do. Fury waited until they were well out of earshot of the wagon before asking the question that was nagging at him.

"Something's wrong, isn't it?"

Joe nodded, his face and voice grim as he replied, "Some of that smoke looks like it's coming from my claim. There's no reason for anybody to be there—unless they're trying to move in and take it over."

"You think it could be the Hellhounds?"

"That's why I wanted J. D. to stay behind us, just in case," Joe said.

The explanation was the same one that had been circulating inside Fury's head, and he agreed that Joe's decision was a good one. If the claim jumpers had already made a move, there was a good chance there'd be shooting before the day was over.

It didn't take long for Fury and Joe to cover the two miles or so to the claim. They followed the bend of the creek as it angled toward the left-hand wall of the canyon, and a few minutes later they could see the spot where the small stream disappeared at the base of the rugged bluff. Now that they were closer, it was obvious that one of the plumes of smoke from a cook fire also had its origin at the same spot.

"Damn it," Joe said fervently. "They've even put up a tent!"

Fury could see it now, a good-sized canvas tent. A small campfire burned in front of it, with a coffeepot staying warm in the ashes at the edge of the fire. Beyond the tent, there were scars on the face of the cliff where somebody had been working with pickaxes. Nobody was in sight at the moment, but as Fury and Joe rode closer and the sound of their horses' hooves could be heard echoing against the wall of the canyon, four men emerged from the tent.

Two of the men carried rifles, while the third one had a scattergun tucked under his arm and the fourth was armed with a brace of pistols strapped around his waist on a cartridge belt. All of them were dressed roughly and sported beards, and they watched Fury and Joe with keen eyes that were touched with suspicion.

As the two riders reined in about ten yards from the claim jumpers, the man with the shotgun came forward a step and called harshly, "That's far enough! What the hell do you want here?"

Fury glanced over at Joe, hoping the young man would keep a tight rein on his temper, at least starting out. It was still possible that these men weren't members of the Hellhounds, that an honest mistake had been made and might be able to be resolved without gunfire. Fury doubted it, but hell, anything was possible, he thought.

Joe's face was taut with anger, but his voice was calm as he replied, "Looks like you gents must be in the wrong place. This is my claim."

"The hell you say!" the spokesman exclaimed. "You're the one who made the mistake, nigger. This is *our* claim." He gave an ugly grin. "Mighty good one, too. Looks like we're gonna make a strike."

Fury recognized the man's Eastern accent and knew that

he must be one of the hard cases from New York who had drifted to San Francisco and wound up in the original Hounds. He wished the other men would say something. If one or more of them talked like an Australian, that would confirm that they were part of the merger between the Hounds and the Sydney Ducks. Nobody was talking, though, except the man with the scattergun.

And his voice had turned ugly again as he went on. "Now clear out o' here before we start shootin'. You been warned, both of you!"

Joe made one final attempt to reason with them. "Listen, I filed on this claim in San Francisco. I've got the paper from the claims office—"

"I don't give a damn about no paper!" The twin barrels of the shotgun started to come up. "Now get the hell out!"

There was no point in delaying things any longer. Fury said quietly and calmly, "I've got the shotgunner, Joe. Pick your own."

Then, as the faces of the four claim jumpers contorted with hate and they started to jerk their guns up, Fury's right hand flashed to the big revolver on his hip.

The dun had heard a lot of gunfire and smelled plenty of powder smoke, and the same was true of Joe's buckskin. Both horses stood still as their riders drew smoothly. At this range the man with the scattergun was the most dangerous, since it didn't take much of an aim to use one of those weapons. Fury went for him first for that reason. The Colt Dragoon boomed and bucked against Fury's palm just as the barrels of the shotgun came level. The heavy ball slammed into the man's chest and drove him backward, and the impact jerked the muzzle of the shotgun up as well. The man was already dead, his heart smashed by Fury's shot, when his finger clenched convulsively on both triggers and sent the double charge of buckshot exploding harmlessly into the sky.

Next to Fury, Joe had his own Colt, a Navy model, spitting fire and lead. It was a smaller caliber, a .36 instead of a .44, but that was plenty big enough to get the job done. Joe's first shot spun around the man who carried two handguns. Both of those pistols were drawn but not yet leveled, and when they blasted, their bullets dug into the ground at their owner's feet. He crumpled, the guns slipping from his lifeless fingers.

One of the men with a rifle got off a shot, the bullet singing over Fury's head. Fury turned a little in the saddle to make himself a smaller target and fired again. The man was knocked backward and landed in a sprawl, his rifle clattering away.

Joe triggered twice at the last man. One of the shots was a clean miss, but the other smashed the man's shoulder and drove him to his knees. He dropped the rifle and grabbed at his injured shoulder with the other hand. As both Fury and Joe lined cocked revolvers on him, he cried, "Don't shoot! Oh, God, don't kill me!"

"Give us a reason not to," Fury suggested coldly.

"I won't cause no more trouble, mate! I promise! Oh, Lord, you've killed me!"

"You'll live . . . maybe. That shoulder'll need some tending to." Fury nodded toward four horses tied up behind the tent. "One of those mounts belong to you?"

"Aye!" the wounded man gasped out.

"Get on him and get out of here," Fury said. "And go back and tell your friends to stay away from this claim."

The man nodded shakily, biting his lips to keep from crying out in pain again. He staggered to his feet, managed to make it to the horses, and untied one of them. Using only one hand, the other arm hanging limp and bloody at his side, he awkwardly pulled himself into the saddle. Banging his heels against the horse's flanks, he got it moving away from the tent and the sprawled corpses of his friends.

Fury and Joe watched him go without holstering their guns. When the man was about fifty yards away, well beyond effective pistol range, he stopped and turned around long enough to yell, "You bastards ain't heard the last o' the Hellhounds!" With that, he urged the horse into a jarring gallop.

For a second, Fury considered pulling his Sharps from the saddleboot and shooting the man off his horse. Then he decided it might be better to let him live and deliver the message he had been given.

"I reckon we're thinking the same thing," Joe said, his hand on the smooth stock of his own carbine. "It's tempting."

"That it is," Fury agreed. "But we want the rest of that bunch to know that we're here and that we don't intend to be run off."

"Damn right."

The wounded Hellhound was out of sight now. Fury slid his Colt back in its holster and said, "We'd better start cleaning up around here. J. D.'ll be here soon."

"Yeah," Joe said, waving a hand toward the bodies. "And I'd just as soon she didn't have to see all this."

Fury and Joe dismounted and dragged the dead men behind the tent, covering them with a piece of canvas they found inside the rough shelter. Fury weighted the canvas down with rocks and said, "That'll do until we can get a grave dug. It won't be anything fancy, not for the likes of them."

Joe snorted. "If there was a good ravine around here, that'd do as far as I'm concerned. I reckon we'll have to plant 'em, though."

Fury gestured out into the canyon. "Looks like we might have some help. Either that, or more trouble on the way."

Joe looked where his companion was indicating and saw several riders converging on the claim. Three of them were coming from farther up the canyon, while a fourth was headed toward them from the far side. After a moment, Fury spotted a wagon, too, following the three riders from the north.

"Doesn't look like trouble," Fury said, shading his eyes from the late afternoon sun. "There's a woman on that wagon, along with the gent driving it."

The single rider from the east arrived first, pulling his horse to a stop and glancing meaningfully at the canvas-covered mound behind the tent. Blood was starting to soak through the canvas in places.

The man wasn't wearing a handgun, but he did have a single-shot rifle in his hands. He was tall, even in the saddle, and wide across the shoulders, with hard blue eyes and a tightly clenched jaw stubbled with a couple of days' growth of dark beard. He nodded toward the covered dead men and said, "Looks like there was some trouble here."

"There sure was," Joe replied. "Claim jumpers tried to take over while I was gone to town. This is my claim. I'm Joe Brackett." He waved a hand. "Light for a spell. . . . That is, if you're not looking for trouble, too."

A friendly grin spread across the visitor's face, softening the grim cast of his features. As he swung down from his saddle, he said, "No, I'm not looking for trouble. Name's Will Corey. I've got a claim on the other side of the canyon. When I heard all the shooting, I figured I'd better come see what was going on."

Fury jerked a thumb at the canvas-covered mound. "There are three of the Hellhounds under there. They didn't want to leave when Joe and I got here. A fourth one wound up with a smashed shoulder. He rode off."

Will Corey nodded. "I think I saw him. Looked like he was swaying in the saddle a mite. Maybe he'll make it to where he's going." Corey looked at Fury. "And who're you?"

"John Fury. I'm a friend of Joe's."

"Part of this claim belong to you, too?"

Fury shook his head. "No, I'm just helping out. Fact is, I work for Alexander Todd, delivering the mail."

Corey's grin widened. "Thank the Lord for Alexander Todd," he said. "Otherwise the miners up here would never hear any news from home or anywhere else. You wouldn't happen to have a letter for me in your pouch, would you?"

"I don't think so," Fury said. "But I'll check later to make sure."

"I'd appreciate it. My claim's straight across the canyon there, like I said." Corey turned his attention back to Joe. "Mr. Brackett, I reckon you've got your papers from the claims office, making everything legal and aboveboard?"

"As a matter of fact, I do," Joe replied. "If it's any of your business."

"No offense intended. It's just that I'm sort of, well, the unofficial mayor of Last Chance Canyon, I guess you'd say. We're getting quite a little community here, even though we're spread out all up and down the canyon, and we're all trying to do things legal-like. Folks picked me to sort of keep an eye on things."

Joe nodded. "I understand. Let me get the papers from my saddlebags."

While he was doing that, the other three riders arrived, followed closely by the wagon. As Fury had noticed, there was indeed a woman on the wagon seat. A girl, really, around eighteen or so, with long red hair. The three young men on horseback were redheaded, as well, and two of them had beards. The family resemblance between them and the girl was obvious. Three brothers and a sister, Fury decided, and the man beside the girl on the wagon seat was likely the father, even though his hair was gray instead of red. He brought the team of mules to a stop, hopped down from the seat, and came over to join Fury, Joe, and Will Corey. He was thick-bodied and a little below medium height.

"Hello, Will," he greeted Corey as he cuffed back his broad-brimmed hat. "What's going on here?"

"Trouble with some claim jumpers," Corey replied. "Hell-hounds, most likely." The mayor of Last Chance Canyon, as he called himself, had looked over the paper from the claims office in San Francisco, and now he nodded at Joe and went on. "This is Joe Brackett. He's the owner of this claim."

The newcomer extended his hand. "Glad to meet you, Joe. I'm Ben Hampton, and this here's my daughter Nora and my boys Dave, Thurl, and Orville. Anytime we can help you out, you just let us know."

"That's mighty friendly of you, Mr. Hampton," Joe said as he shook hands with the man. The three Hampton sons nudged their horses over and leaned down from their saddles to shake hands, too. Dave and Thurl were the oldest, in their early twenties, and had beards. Orville was around sixteen, which made him the youngest of the bunch.

Fury recognized the name Hampton, and as soon as Joe had performed the introductions, he said, "I think I've got some mail for you, Mr. Hampton. I seem to remember seeing a couple of letters in the pouch with your name on them."

Hampton's grin broadened. "Well, that's mighty fine news. We've got good neighbors here in the canyon, but we still like to hear from the folks back home."

"Where's that?" asked Fury.

"Western Virginia. Used to drive a freight wagon back and forth 'cross the Alleghenies. That's mighty poor country, though, so me and the young'uns came out here to make our fortune." Hampton laughed. "We ain't done it yet, but we're tryin'. Nothin' to go back to in Virginny."

"I knew a man from Virginia," Joe said cautiously. "His name was Nate Boyd. Not a bad sort, I reckon, but he came from a plantation, and we didn't get along too well at first."

" 'Cause you're a darkie?" Hampton shook his head. "Don't worry none about that, Joe. Wasn't many slaves in our part of the state, and we never held with it. Just about everybody west of the Alleghenies was too poor to have slaves. You'll get along just fine here."

Will Corey pointed back down the canyon. "Somebody else coming."

"That's my partner with our supplies," Joe said. He lifted his hat and waved J. D. on, so that she would know the group of people gathered on the claim meant no harm.

Nora Hampton exclaimed, "That's a lady drivin' that wagon!" Obviously, she wasn't accustomed to seeing other females here in Last Chance Canyon.

J. D. brought the wagon to a stop and looked around curiously at the strangers. Her gaze stopped on the bloody, canvas-covered forms behind the tent. "I knew I heard shooting," she said. "What happened, Joe? Were the Hellhounds here?"

"That's their tent," Joe said. "They weren't of a mind to leave, even when I explained this was my claim."

J. D. stepped down lithely from the wagon before Fury could go over to help her. Instinctively, he made a move in her direction, though, and he noticed that Will Corey did the same thing.

Joe introduced J. D. to everyone, and then Corey said in a tone of disbelief, "You came up here to help Mr. Brackett work the claim, Mrs. McKavett?"

"Well, I hadn't intended to," J. D. explained. "But my store in San Francisco burned down, and practically all I had left in the world were those supplies we'd already loaded on the wagon. If I'm ever going to rebuild my business, this claim is going to have to pay off. So I want to do everything in my power to see that it does, even if it means swinging a pick and panning for gold myself."

"That's mighty admirable, ma'am," Hampton told her. "And I know Nora'll be happy to have another lady in the canyon. This is a mighty lonely place for a gal all alone."

Fury reached into the wagon and brought out a shovel. "I'm going to get started on a grave," he grunted. "Those Hellhounds aren't going to be getting any more fragrant."

"The boys'll give you a hand," Hampton said. "We got shovels in the wagon." He motioned for his sons to help Fury dig the grave.

Will Corey didn't pitch in, Fury noticed. Instead, Corey took his hat off and started talking in a low voice to J. D. She smiled and laughed, and Fury supposed Corey was just being friendly. Fury frowned and wondered if he was feeling jealous. There was no reason to, he told himself. He wasn't the least bit romantically interested in J. D. McKavett, although he did admire her determination and the way she was trying to bounce back from the tragic fire that had destroyed her business.

With Fury, Joe, and all three of the Hampton boys working on the grave, it didn't take long to scoop out a big enough hole for the dead Hellhounds, even in this hard, rocky ground. After wrapping the corpses in the canvas which had covered them, Fury and Joe rolled the bodies into the grave. "I ain't saying words over them," Joe declared as he straightened from the grisly task.

Will Corey stepped forward. "I'll do it," he said. "Even low-down scum like that deserve a decent send-off into the next life."

While the onlookers took off their hats, Corey intoned a brief prayer, then said loudly, "Amen." The others echoed that sentiment, and with the short service over, Fury and his helpers began tossing dirt back in the hole.

Joe leaned over and hefted the coffeepot. "Near full," he announced. "Reckon we might as well enjoy the hospitality of the gents who used to live here."

J. D. fetched cups from the wagon and poured coffee for everyone. The shadows of twilight were settling down by now, and Ben Hampton said, "Be night soon. You folks are welcome to come over to our claim for supper if you want."

"I'll be getting back to my own spot, Ben, but thanks for the offer," Corey said. "Good night, gents. And good night to you, Mrs. McKavett."

"Good night, Mr. Corey," J. D. murmured.

"I think we'd better stick around here, too," Joe said when Corey had mounted up and ridden off. "I don't reckon any of the Hellhounds will be back tonight, but you never can tell."

"True enough," Hampton agreed. "Well, the offer stands open, anytime you'd care to take us up on it."

"We'll do that," Joe promised.

Fury said, "Before you go, Mr. Hampton, there's something I'm curious about. You've been here for a while, haven't you?"

" 'Bout as long as anybody in these parts, I reckon," Hampton replied.

"Why do they call it Last Chance Canyon?"

Hampton rubbed his jaw and thought for a moment before answering. Finally, he said, "Don't know who put that handle on the place, but I reckon it fits. I quit my job and sold my land back East, and it took all the money we could scrape together to make the trip out here. When I said before there was nothin' to go back to, I meant it. We either make it here, or we don't make it at all. Will Corey's in the same boat. Sold everything he had and came West to look for gold. Don't know what he'll do if he don't find it. Same holds true for just about everybody else in the canyon."

J. D. said, "I understand what you mean, Mr. Hampton. Everything I have is right here." She waved her hand to take in the claim. "This is my last chance, too."

"Good Lord willin', it'll pay off for all of us." Hampton tugged on the brim of his hat. "Well, good night, ma'am. Good night, boys."

With friendly waves, the Hamptons rode off into the dusk. Fury, Joe, and J. D. watched them go.

For a drifter like him, thought Fury, there was always another chance, and there would be until the day he wound up in a lonely, unmarked grave somewhere—like those Hellhounds. But J. D. was different, and maybe Joe was, too.

For their sake, Fury hoped they found what they were looking for here in Last Chance Canyon.

CHAPTER
9

Just as he had thought, Fury had letters in one of the mail pouches for Ben Hampton. He dug them out of the pouch that night, after they had eaten the meal that Joe cooked, and slipped them into his saddlebag so that he wouldn't have any trouble finding them when he paid a visit to the Hampton claim.

"What are we going to do about that tent?" J. D. asked.

Fury shrugged. "If nobody comes to claim it, I reckon it belongs to you and Joe. It's on your property."

J. D. hugged herself as a little shudder of revulsion ran through her. "I don't know if I'd feel comfortable sleeping in a tent that used to belong to dead men, and bandits at that."

"We'll boil their blankets and gear," Joe decided, "to get rid of any vermin they left behind. But there's nothing wrong with the tent. You take it, J. D., until we can get a cabin put up."

With a reluctant nod, J. D. agreed. "I guess I can do that. It'll be nicer than sleeping underneath the wagon."

As soon as they had cleaned out the tent, Fury and Joe spread their bedrolls on the ground outside, as usual, and Fury took the first watch. He sat well away from the faintly glowing campfire, his back propped against a rock. From what he had seen of the Hellhounds, they wouldn't be above sneaking back up to the claim and taking a potshot at him, so he stayed out of the small circle of light cast by the fire and kept his eyes and ears open.

Nobody showed up to bother him, and the rest of the night was quiet as well, Joe reported the next morning. Fury lingered over the breakfast of coffee, bacon, and corn bread, then said, "I've still got some mail deliveries to make for Alexander Todd. I'd better go ahead and take care of that now, since it'll likely take the Hellhounds a few days to decide what to do next."

"I can tell you what they'll do," Joe said grimly. "They'll come back and try to take over the claim. They're not going to give up, John."

"I know that." Fury nodded. "That's why as soon as I've finished dropping off the rest of the mail, I'm going to take the pouches over to Sonora and turn them over to Todd's man, along with my resignation. I enjoyed the job, but I'm needed here."

"Thanks, John," Joe said sincerely. "I reckon we can manage all right until you get back, but I've got to admit I'll be glad to see you again."

"I'll get around as quick as I can," Fury promised.

A little later, he saddled the dun, said good-bye to Joe and J. D., and rode out, heading north toward Ben Hampton's claim. He found it on the far side of the canyon about mid-morning.

Thurl Hampton was chipping away at the side of a bluff as Fury rode up. The day was already pretty warm, and Thurl had taken his shirt off. His fair skin was already blistered from other days of working in the hot sun. The red-bearded young man nodded to Fury and grinned. "Pa and Nora are in the cabin," he called. "The other boys have gone up around the bend to work."

Fury lifted a hand in a wave of acknowledgment, then reined up in front of a good-sized log cabin. It was sturdily constructed, Fury saw, and if nothing else, the Hamptons had built themselves a good place to live. People still had to eat, however, and this was no country for farming. The payoff had to come out of the ground, but it would be gold, not green.

Ben Hampton emerged with the usual friendly grin on his face, followed by his daughter. "Mornin', Mr. Fury," he said. "You bring that mail?"

"Sure did," Fury said, taking the letters from his saddlebag and handing them to Hampton. "I'm supposed to collect an ounce of dust for each of them."

"I know. Got it together last night. Fetch it from the cabin, Nora." Hampton looked up at Fury. "That'll put a dent in our poke, but shoot, a man's got to get his mail, don't he? And it'd cost me more to go all the way down to Frisco and get it myself. Can't afford to send one of the boys, either. It takes all of us workin' every day to scratch out a livin'. Goin' to be better someday, though, when we hit a good vein."

"I hope you do, Mr. Hampton."

"Call me Ben. Here's Nora with the dust." Hampton took the small leather pouch from the girl and gave it to Fury. "You got a scale so's you can weigh that?"

Fury balanced the poke on the palm of his hand. "Close enough," he judged. "Todd hired me to deliver the mail, not to weigh every little smidgen of dust like an assayer." He stowed away the payment, then nodded and touched the brim of his hat. "I'll be riding on. Got other letters to deliver."

Hampton had already torn open the seals on the two letters, and now he handed them to Nora. "I don't have the book-learnin' to read 'em myself, but Nora does. Thanks, Mr. Fury, and so long."

Fury turned the dun and rode away with a wave. Behind him, Nora Hampton was reading the letters to her father, and both of them were smiling.

There were three more letters for miners who had claims here in Last Chance Canyon, and Fury located them and delivered the messages before the day was over. When he had done that, he studied the map Todd had given him and decided to follow the trail that meandered away from the north end of the canyon. It would take him to a settlement called Broadax, and he had mail for people who lived there.

One man couldn't hope to cover the vast sprawl of the Sierra Nevada by himself, and Fury understood why Todd had quite a few riders and several local agents working for him. It would take Fury another day or two to complete his swing through the mountains, and then he would head back past Last Chance Canyon and over to Sonora. That would give him a chance to check on Joe and J. D. before he turned over the outgoing mail and the money and gold dust he had collected to the express company's agent.

From Broadax, Fury circled back to the west, visiting Volcano, Rich Gulch, and Dogtown before starting once more toward Last Chance Canyon. The names and locations of the rough-and-tumble mining camps all blended into one another as Fury stopped in them to deliver the mail. After two days on the trail, the pouches were noticeably emptier of letters, but he had collected a sizable amount of gold dust, coins, and even a few pieces of folding money. This was going to be a profitable trip for Alexander Todd, and Fury would collect some decent wages from the agent in Sonora, too.

He hoped that the Hellhounds hadn't come back to the claim to harass Joe and J. D. Joe Brackett could take care of himself, of course; Fury knew that from experience. And J. D. had proven during the fire in San Francisco that she was levelheaded enough not to panic during an emergency. Still, Fury would feel better about things once he had finished this chore for Todd and returned to the claim to join his friends.

His study of the map had told him that the creek originating in Last Chance Canyon was a tributary of the Calaveras River, and he hit the river itself south of Dogtown. All he had to do was follow it to where the creek branched off, then that trail would take him back to the canyon. This wasn't the way he and Joe and J. D. had approached the place the first time. That route was a little south of his current position, since they had followed the broad valley between the Calaveras River and the Stanislaus River on their way out from San Francisco. But Fury was confident that this trail would take him where he wanted to go.

As he rode along beside the brawling, fast-flowing river, tall wooded bluffs rose on each side of the stream. Fury kept an eye on them. From the time he had rolled out of his blankets this morning, there had been a faint prickle on the back of his neck, an almost sure sign that someone was watching him. It might not mean anything. Could be just a curious miner tagging along. Sometimes these men were so isolated up here in the mountains that they got leery of strangers, and it might take one of them all day to work up enough gumption to approach a fellow traveler and start up a conversation.

There were more likely explanations for the feeling, though, and Fury was well aware of them. There could be bandits on his trail, like the men who had ambushed Johnny Phipps. Or it could be members of the Hellhounds looking for revenge for their dead companions. Fury couldn't be certain what was going on.

But he was ready for trouble if it came.

Or at least he thought he was. What he wasn't ready for was half of a mountain falling on him.

That was what it seemed like. There was a sudden rumbling noise from the top of the bluff to Fury's left, and when he jerked his gaze in that direction, he saw several boulders bounding toward him, bringing with them a plunging torrent of smaller rocks. The avalanche was spreading out in front of him, and he knew there was no way he could outrun it in the direction he had been going.

He hauled the dun's head around and slammed his heels into its flanks. Backtracking was his only chance, and it was a slim one.

The dun's powerful muscles corded and rippled as it surged into a gallop. Fury leaned forward in the saddle, urging every bit of speed out of the animal that he possibly could. He yanked his hat off and slapped it against the dun's rump as the noise of the avalanche grew into an overpowering roar. Pebbles falling out in front of the landslide began to pelt both man and horse.

Then, abruptly, they were out of the path of the slide. Boulders crashed to the bank of the river behind them, but Fury and the dun were safe. Fury reined in and turned the horse around to survey the damage as a few final rocks came clattering down the slope. It had been a close call, thought Fury, a damned close one.

A gun blasted above him.

Fury jerked in the saddle in surprise, but the bullet didn't come anywhere near him. And a second later, even as he was lifting his eyes to search for the source of the shot, a harsh cry of alarm reached his ears.

Up at the top of the bluff, more dirt had given way, no doubt weakened by the avalanche. A man had been standing there at the edge when it collapsed, Fury saw, and it had to be the man who had taken the shot at him when the landslide failed to engulf him. Now the man was clinging desperately to a small bush just below the rim, and that was the only thing keeping him from plunging down the almost sheer slope below him. Such a fall would more than likely be fatal.

"Damn it!" Fury muttered as he recognized the clothes of the man hanging from the edge of the cliff. "Milo Phipps again!"

It was Milo, all right. The gangling figure was unmistakable. Fury had begun to think that Milo had given up his unreasonable grudge and gone back to San Francisco, but obviously he'd been wrong. Milo's streak of bad luck was still going strong, however. Not only had the landslide he'd started failed to get Fury, but he himself had wound up in bad trouble because of it when he came to the edge of the bluff to try another rifle shot.

Milo was howling in fear and trying to scramble back up to the top of the bluff, but there weren't enough places where he could get a foothold. Fury frowned as he looked up at the former express rider. Milo wasn't going to be able to hang on to his precarious perch much longer. All Fury had to do was cross the river, follow the opposite bank, and ride off.

That would solve the problem of Milo Phipps. Even if the fall didn't kill Milo, he would be hurt too badly to think about following Fury anymore. He'd probably die from his injuries, in fact, right there in the rubble of the avalanche beside the river.

Fury sat there on the dun for a long few seconds, then heaved a sigh and uttered a heartfelt, "Damnation!" Then he tilted his head back and called up, "Hang on, Milo! I'll come give you a hand!"

The bluff was not quite so steep where Fury was. If he could get to the top of it and then work his way along the rim, he would soon reach a spot where he could pull Milo back to safety. But as he dismounted and started walking quickly toward the slope, Fury wondered just how crazy for revenge Milo really was. Would he take advantage of the opportunity to grab Fury's hand and pull both of them over the cliff?

Fury supposed he would just have to take that chance. He knew he couldn't ride off and leave Milo to die, not without at least trying to help him.

Selecting his handholds and footholds carefully, Fury began to climb. The bluff was rugged enough here, with plenty of outcroppings of rock, so that he had little trouble scaling it. Over where Milo was, though, the landslide had pretty well scoured the face of the bluff clean except for a few tattered outgrowths of brush, and the fragile roots of one of those were the only things saving Milo from a bad fall of fifty or sixty feet.

It took Fury only a few minutes to reach the top of the bluff. He hurried along it, and when he reached the spot where Milo had fallen, he took his hat off and went to his knees to peer over the edge.

Milo was about three feet below him and a little to the right. Keeping his voice steady and calm, Fury told him, "Hang on, boy, and I'll get you back up here."

Milo stopped yelling and lifted wide eyes to meet Fury's gaze. "Help me," he pleaded.

"I'm going to." Fury stretched out full-length on his stomach, his head and shoulders extending past the edge of the bluff. He reached down with his right arm, stretching his hand out as far as he could. "You're going to have to pull yourself up a little and reach up to me, Milo."

"I . . . I can't! I can't move!"

"You've got to." Fury's voice grew harder as he went on. "This is the second time you've tried to kill me, and I'm getting damned tired of it. It'd serve you right if I got on my horse and rode away—"

"No!"

"Then reach up here and take my hand, blast it!" Fury snapped. "That bush you're hanging on to is going to pull loose sooner or later."

In fact, the roots of the bush did seem to be shifting a little, loosening their grip on the soil. Small clods of dirt let go around the base of it and pattered down on Milo's head and shoulders. Fury figured the bush might last another couple of minutes at the most, and then it was going to give way.

"Come on!" he urged. "Now!"

Milo swallowed hard and then shifted his grip on the bush a little, getting himself ready for the effort. Fury managed to reach out another couple of inches toward him, but that was the absolute limit. If he edged out any more, he was liable to topple over the rim himself. Of course, that might be just what Milo wanted. . . .

With a grunt, Milo pulled himself up and then let go with his right hand, reaching desperately for Fury's hand. Fury's fingers closed around the young man's wrist, tightening as Milo started to slip back down. Milo let out a yell as the roots of the bush gave way with a shower of dirt. His weight hit Fury's arm and shoulders. The strain washed through Fury, but he dug into the ground with his other hand and the sharp toes of his boots and managed to hang on.

"Grab something else, damn it!" Fury said. "You've got to help me, Milo, or I can't pull you up!"

Milo's frantically scrabbling fingertips found a tiny out-cropping of rock. It wasn't much, but as he latched on to it, that eased enough of the strain on his rescuer so that Fury was able to pull him up a bit more.

"Reach for the rim!" Fury ordered.

Milo hesitated, obviously scared to let go of even the smallest handhold, but after a second he lunged up again, and this time his hand closed over the edge of the bluff.

Fury hauled upward with all the strength he could summon. Milo's toes found the wall of the bluff and pushed against it. He rose high enough so that Fury was able to reach forward with his left hand and hook it under Milo's right arm. Then Fury surged backward, pulling hard. Milo came up and over the rim, falling forward to sprawl on top of him as Fury fell back.

"Get off me, blast it!" Fury shouted, his voice muffled by Milo's scrawny form.

Milo rolled to the side and lay on his back, chest heaving as he sucked in huge breaths of air. Fury sat up beside him, gulped down a few breaths himself, and then drew the big Dragoon from its holster. As he thumbed back the hammer, Fury put the muzzle of the gun against Milo's head.

"I'd hate to kill somebody I just risked my life to save," Fury said, "but I'll sure as hell do it unless you can convince me there won't be any more bushwhacking. You've got about a minute, boy, and then I pull the trigger."

Milo blinked rapidly and stared up at him. "D-don't shoot!" he gasped. "I'm sorry, Mr. Fury! God, I'm sorry!"

"You started that landslide, didn't you?"

Milo's head moved in a miniscule nod.

"And then when that didn't work, you took another shot at me." Fury shook his head in disgust. "Lord, I reckon my brain's gone soft. I *should've* ridden off and left you out there on that cliff."

Tears welled out of Milo's eyes and cut little trails in the dust that coated his cheeks. "I said I was sorry! I'll never do it again! I guess I can't do *anything* right. . . ."

Fury looked down at him for a few seconds, then took the gun away from his head. He uncocked and holstered the Colt and started to laugh. Falling back on the ground, Fury looked up at the sky above them and whooped and howled with laughter. After a minute, Milo began laughing, too.

There were tears in Fury's eyes when he finally sat up, but they were tears of hilarity. He wiped them away and said, "Boy, if there was ever a sorrier case than you, I never saw him. I'm surprised you didn't shoot your own foot off one of those times when you were gunning for me."

Milo hiccuped a couple of times. "Yeah, I reckon you're right," he said. "But what am I going to do now? You saved my life. I can't keep trying to kill you."

"You could get some sense in that stupid head of yours and believe what I told you about how your brother died," Fury told him.

The mention of Johnny Phipps's death sobered both of them. Milo sat up, wiped his eyes with the back of his hand, and said, "You're right. I've been a damned fool. If you were the kind of man I thought you were, you wouldn't have helped somebody who just tried to dump a ton of rocks on your head." He looked over at Fury. "I'm truly sorry."

Fury got to his feet, brushed himself off, then offered a hand to the young man. "Just don't do it again," he said.

"I won't. You got my word on that, Mr. Fury." Milo's usual hangdog look reappeared on his face. "But what am I going to do now? I lost my job, and I wasn't any good at mining. Hell, I wasn't even any good at revenge."

Fury's brain was working, and as a possibility suggested itself to him, he asked, "When you and your brother were prospecting, did you ever find any gold?"

"Nary a bit. Not one damned sign of color, anywhere we looked."

"Then you were just unlucky," Fury told him. "You don't know how things would've worked out if you'd actually found gold. You might've done just fine as a miner."

"Well, maybe," Milo said dubiously.

"My friend Joe has a claim, and it's certain sure there's gold on it. He could probably use some help getting it out of there. He's got vein and dust both. One of you could work on the stream while the other was chipping out nuggets with a pick."

Milo's face started to light up a little. "You think so?"

"I think so," Fury said. "Besides, he's got some other trouble on his plate, and it wouldn't hurt to have an extra gun around the place." Fury frowned at him. "Even if you haven't hit anything you've aimed at yet."

"I could try to do better," Milo said earnestly.

For a second, Fury thought he was going to start laughing again, but then he settled down. Milo was being so blasted sincere, he would probably take offense if he thought Fury was hoorawing him. Fury put his hand on the youngster's shoulder and said, "All right, you come along with me. I'm on my way back to Last Chance Canyon now. You can stay there and help out on the claim while I run these mail pouches over to Sonora. After that, we'll see how you're doing. How's that sound to you?"

"That sounds fine, Mr. Fury, mighty fine. And I swear I'll never try to kill you again."

"You remember that," Fury said dryly.

As they found Milo's horse and mounted up, Fury thought that considering what Milo had managed to accomplish so far, Last Chance Canyon was living up to its name one more time.

CHAPTER
10
....

Fury had been gone from the claim for two days, and Joe and J. D. had been busy during that time. Joe had intended to start work on a cabin, but the temptation to go ahead and begin making his fortune was too great. Besides, as long as the weather held, he didn't mind sleeping outside, and J. D. had the tent to use.

J. D. was a willing worker, and on the morning that Fury left, she and Joe constructed a long tom sluice from some of the boards they had brought in the wagon. A long, shallow, slanting, box-like contraption, the long tom was placed in the creek itself so that water was constantly running through it. Once it was in position, Joe showed J. D. how to stand on the edge of the stream and lift shovelfuls of dirt from the bottom of the creekbed. The dirt was tossed through the open top of the long tom, where the water washed it to the other end. Along the way, though, small ledges on the bottom of the box called riffles caught the small specks of gold dust, which were heavier than the rest of the sand and gravel with which they were intermingled. It was a simple system that could be worked by one person, rather than the two or three required for the operation of a cradle, which also washed gold dust out of dirt, and much more efficient than the old-fashioned method of panning for gold.

Once J. D. had mastered the operation of the long tom, Joe took pick and shovel and headed for the bluff itself. "No way of knowing how much gold's in there," he told J. D. "Could be just a few nuggets, could be a rich lode. Only way to find out is to start chipping away at it."

J. D. leaned on her shovel on the creekbank. "Go ahead," she said. "I can handle this."

Joe had to grin a little. She looked and sounded confident in a long skirt and a shirt with the sleeves rolled halfway up her bare arms. Her blond hair was tied back behind her head so that it would stay out of her way. There was an eager expression on her face. By the time she'd thrown a few hundred shovelfuls of dirt into the long tom by day's end, Joe thought, she wouldn't be so enthusiastic about this endeavor.

But it would pay off. He was sure of that, and so was J. D. And nobody except overly optimistic Easterners had ever said mining for gold was easy. . . .

Over the next two days, they found out just how difficult it was. J. D. shoveled dirt from the creekbed and threw it into the long tom until her back felt like it was going to snap in two every time she bent over. Blisters formed on her hands and burst, making the handle of the shovel slippery with fluid. She didn't waste energy crying, though. Her hands would harden and calluses would form, and muscles she had never used before that were now shrieking in agony with every movement would become stronger and able to take more punishment. Her future, her very life, was in that stream, and if she had to filter it out speck by gleaming speck, that was what she was going to do.

As for Joe, he swung the pick for endless hours, the sharp steel implement hitting the rock with a distinctive *chink* that made a kind of crude music. Music to get rich by, if a man was lucky. But it was hard work, every bit as backbreaking and blister-raising as shoveling dirt into the long tom. When Joe had a good-sized pile of rock chipped off the wall, he shoveled it up and put it in a small wheeled cart that had also been brought out from San Francisco on the wagon. He trundled the cart away from the wall of the canyon, taking it over to a nice flat spot where he could spread the rocks out on the ground. One by one, he went through the pieces, looking for the golden gleam sought after by so many men. Sometimes when he found it he was able to take his knife blade and pry the placer gold away from the rock to which it was bonded. In some cases, though, the gold was too intermixed with the quartz to be worked out, and then Joe had to take a hammer and smash the chunks of rock into fine gravel from which the gold could be picked out. It was tedious work, and alternating between that and swinging the pick produced a state of utter exhaustion.

It was going to be worth it, though, Joe told himself. He tossed the bits of gold he found into a tin cup, and each *clink* as the precious metal landed meant more money in his pocket sooner or later.

At the end of the first day, when they had put in only the afternoon and a little bit of the morning after finishing the long tom, Joe got out the scales and found that they had two and a half pounds of nuggets and another twelve ounces of dust.

"What does that work out to?" Joe asked anxiously as J. D. did the calculation in her head.

"If my storekeeper's arithmetic hasn't failed me, that's about eight hundred and thirty-six dollars worth of gold." J. D.'s voice was low and full of awe. She repeated slowly, "Eight hundred and thirty-six."

Joe let out a whistle. "I reckon that's more money than I've seen before in my whole life put together," he said. "We're going to be rich, J. D., rich!"

"I know. I can hardly believe it!"

Neither of them really knew what they were doing as the knowledge of impending wealth struck them. Suddenly they were on their feet, hand in blistered hand, dancing around the camp, jumping up and down, and letting out joyous whoops, their sore muscles forgotten for the moment. Joe's assessment of the claim's potential had been correct. There was gold here, and plenty of it.

Just as abruptly as they had started their celebration, they stopped short and stood there, blinking a little as they stared at each other in the fading light of dusk. Joe said, "Ah . . ."

J. D. slipped her fingers out of his. "I guess we got a little carried away," she said, looking down at the ground. "We'd better start thinking about fixing something for supper."

"You mean we'd better think about *me* fixing something," Joe said with a chuckle. "I've eaten your cooking, remember?"

She took a mock swipe at his head, and he ducked away grinning. "It wasn't that bad," J. D. said.

"It wasn't good."

"I'll gather some wood for a fire."

"You do that."

Joe went to the wagon and started poking among the provisions. They needed something special to celebrate their first day of working the claim and also the over eight hundred dollars worth of gold they had taken out of the ground and the creek. He found some canned peaches and nodded. Out here on the frontier, canned peaches were the ultimate treat, and they'd do just fine for a little informal gold-finding party.

He got out some salt pork and biscuit makings, too, and started back to where J. D. was building a fire. As he went, he scanned the walls of the canyon. Everything was quiet this evening, and there had been no sign of the Hellhounds all day. They had to know how valuable the claim was, though. There was no telling, in fact, how much gold the claim jumpers had taken out before Fury, Joe, and J. D. had shown up to run them off. Sooner or later, they would make a move again. Joe was sure of that, and he couldn't allow himself to become so euphoric over the newfound riches that he let his guard down.

"We'll have to split the watches tonight," he said over supper. "Somebody's got to stand guard all the time."

"Well, I should hope so," J. D. responded. "I was rather put out with you and John for not letting me take my turn while we were on the way up here. I'm perfectly capable, you know."

"I'm not disputing that. I've got an extra six-gun and shell belt you can use, and there's a couple of extra carbines."

"Don't worry about me," J. D. assured him. "I'll be fine."

She chose the first watch, and after they had eaten, Joe got the spare revolver and holster from the wagon. He showed her how to load it, then watched as she buckled the cartridge belt around her waist.

"How do I look?" she asked.

"Just fine," he said. Actually, he thought it looked rather ludicrous for a woman to be wearing a gun like that, but he kept the thought to himself, knowing that J. D. wouldn't take it kindly. Then he handed her one of the carbines and some spare cartridges, which she dropped in the pocket of her skirt.

"I'm ready," J. D. declared. "You can turn in whenever you want."

"You're sure about this?"

"I'm positive. Get some rest, Joe. You need it." J. D. knelt beside the fire and poured herself another cup of coffee. "Don't worry about a thing."

"All right. But you wake me up round midnight, you hear?"

"Of course."

While Joe rolled up in his blankets and tipped his hat down over his eyes, J. D. carried her cup of coffee over to the wagon and sat down on the ground with her back against one of the wheels. Fury had told her about not remaining too close to the fire when you were standing guard, and he had warned her as well to keep her eyes moving and never to let them settle on the flames. There was something hypnotic about a fire at night that could make you miss other things going on around you. Not only that, but your eyes got used to the light, and then you couldn't see nearly as well if you had to look at something in the darkness or, say, aim a gun off into the shadows. Fury had told her about that, too.

She had a feeling there were a great many things a woman could learn from John Fury.

J. D. smiled a little at that thought. Fury was attractive enough, in a rawboned, weathered way, and he possessed an air of utter competence that was compelling. But while J. D. liked him well enough, she couldn't honestly say that she harbored any romantic feelings for him.

It had been a long time since her husband had died, and she had known a lot of loneliness since then. Given the right circumstances, who was to say what she might do?

J. D. drew a deep breath and told herself sternly not to let her thoughts start straying like that again. She should be thinking about the Hellhounds and the danger they represented, not John Fury.

Despite her assurances to Joe that she would be all right, the silence of the night began to get to her. Not that it was all that silent, she reflected. There were all sorts of rustlings and scurryings in the brush and an owl hooted somewhere nearby, then cut through the night with a flapping of wings as it went in search of prey. A coyote howled in the distance. There could be all manner of things out there, J. D. realized, some friendly, some hostile, some indifferent, and she might not even know about it until they were right on top of her. It was impossible to listen for *everything*. . . .

With an effort of will, J. D. got a grip on herself and waited until her wildly thudding pulse had slowed down. Then she stood up and walked quietly around the camp, thinking that taking a look around might make her feel a bit less nervous.

"I don't reckon it's time for my watch yet, is it?"

J. D. jumped and gave a gasp of surprise as Joe spoke. "Did I wake you?" she asked. "I didn't mean to. I was just looking around."

He lifted his head a little and pushed his hat back up so that he could look at her. "Did you hear anything?"

"Not really. I was just . . ." J. D. shrugged. "Looking around, like I said."

Joe tipped his hat forward again. "All right. But remind me to teach you about walking quiet when we get the chance."

J. D. swallowed her irritation at his smug tone and said, "Of course. Everything's fine, so you can go back to sleep."

"I'll try," Joe said.

He could be infuriating, J. D. thought, just like Fury. She supposed all men had that trait in common.

The night passed quietly. She woke Joe at midnight, then went into the tent and slid gratefully into her bedroll. After the long day of labor, even the hard ground felt good, and J. D. dropped off to sleep almost right away.

When Joe woke her in the morning, her muscles were so stiff and sore she could barely move. As she hobbled out of the tent, a groan escaped from her lips.

"Wish I could tell you it's going to get better," Joe said from where he crouched beside the fire, cooking bacon. "But it ain't. Not for a while, anyway."

"I'll be all right," J. D. told him stubbornly. "I'll just think about all that gold, and then it won't hurt as much."

"Worth a try," he said. "In the meantime, have some coffee."

J. D. felt a little more human after she had eaten breakfast and swallowed three cups of Joe's strong coffee. As for the former scout, he was tired, too, but he'd been leading an active, outdoor life for many years, so the hard work on the claim didn't affect him as much as it did J. D. By a half hour after sunup, he was back at work, and so was J. D., although she was shoveling and tossing the dirt into the long tom a little slower today.

The morning's work went well. When the sun was straight overhead at noon, Joe called a halt and was about to rustle up some food for them when he spotted someone coming. A wagon rolled over the rough floor of the canyon, and at the reins of the team was Ben Hampton. Nora sat beside him.

"Howdy!" called the former freighter as he brought the wagon to a stop. "We brought you some grub."

Nora hopped down from the seat with the agility of youth and lifted a straw basket from the back of the wagon. As she brought it over and handed it to J. D., she said, "We remember how hard it was getting started working on a claim. Maybe this'll help a little."

J. D. lifted the red and white checked cloth that was spread over the top of the basket, and her eyes widened in surprise at the sight of fried chicken, fresh greens, and biscuits. She asked, "Where did you get all of this?"

"Got a little garden patch out behind our shack," Hampton explained. "It ain't much—ground's too rocky for that. But we grow a few vegetables and raise a chicken or two. Man gets tired of eatin' salt pork and beans."

"He sure does," Joe agreed enthusiastically. "You two are going to join us, aren't you?"

"Don't mind if we do," Hampton said as he climbed down from the wagon.

The meal was enjoyable. The food was good, Hampton spun several amusing yarns about his family's life back in Virginia, and by the end of the visit, Joe and J. D. felt like they had really been welcomed into the scattered community growing up here in Last Chance Canyon.

Hampton and Nora climbed back onto the wagon and drove off with friendly waves, and J. D. said, "Those are nice folks."

"Yep," Joe agreed. "You notice Ben didn't ask us how much gold we were taking out of the claim?"

"Yes, I did, and it surprised me. I would have thought he'd be curious."

"Oh, he's curious, all right," Joe said. "But he's too polite to ask just yet. Wouldn't want to look like he was jealous of our claim. I reckon he'll get around to it when he knows us better."

Although it pained her to stand up, J. D. did so. "Well, I guess we'd better get back to work."

"Good idea. That gold's not going to jump up out of the ground at us."

Joe was walking toward the canyon wall when a sudden clattering sound ahead of him made him look up. As he did so, he spotted a figure trying to jerk back out of sight up on the rimrock. Warning bells went off in Joe's brain.

"J. D.!" he shouted, dropping the pick and shovel and reaching for the gun on his hip. "Get down!"

More figures appeared at the top of the canyon wall, and rifles started to crack. Now that one of the men had clumsily knocked off a rock that had gone bouncing down the slope, there was no longer any chance of surprise. The bushwhackers opened up, sending bullets screaming around Joe, kicking up dust at his feet.

The wagon was nearby, and he flung himself toward it, seeking its shelter. Something tugged his hat right off his head, and he knew it had been a bullet coming within an inch or two of killing him. Then he hit the hard ground behind the wagon, and for the moment at least, he had a little cover.

Over at the creek, J. D. splashed into the water, gasping for breath as the icy cold of the stream hit her. The creek bubbled up out of the rocks at the base of the canyon wall, but farther up in the mountains, it was fed by melting snow, and it lost little of its frigidity as it made its tortuous way down slope. J. D. headed for the long tom and crouched behind its framework. The apparatus wouldn't provide much cover, but it was better than nothing. She was still wearing the six-gun belted around her waist, and she drew the weapon before bending even lower. As far as she could tell, the men up on the bluff weren't shooting at her but were instead concentrating their fire on Joe.

That was their mistake, J. D. thought grimly. She lifted the heavy revolver, pulled back the hammer with both thumbs, and steadied the barrel on the frame of the long tom. After a moment, when one of the ambushers lifted himself into plain sight in an effort to get a better shot at Joe, J. D. settled the blade of the gun sight on his bulky figure and pressed the trigger.

Close up like this, the roar of the gun was louder than she expected, and its recoil almost sent her falling over backward into the creek. She caught her balance in time to see the man she had aimed at double over and fall forward off the canyon wall, plummeting loosely down to the ground.

Sickness punched J. D. in the belly. She could tell from the way the man had fallen that he was dead. She had just killed a man, ended his life forever. The thought was enough to make the world swim dizzily before her eyes.

She blinked to clear her vision, shoved the queasiness in her stomach away with an effort of will. The man had been doing his damnedest to kill Joe, and once Joe had been disposed of, they would come after her. She didn't need to waste any sympathy on him.

Especially now that the hidden gunmen were turning some of their attention on her. She had made herself a threat by shooting down one of them, and now they were answering. Bullets thudded into the long tom near her head.

Joe scuttled under the wagon and poked his head out on the far side just enough to snap a couple of shots up toward the rimrock. He couldn't tell if they did any good because he had to pull back quickly from the return fire. They had him pinned down but good, and although the heavy planks of the wagon would stop some of the bullets, others would penetrate. It was only a matter of time until one of those shots found him.

He couldn't stay here, but there was no better cover around. Even if there had been, those boys up on the rimrock would cut him down as soon as he made a run for it. The Hellhounds—and Joe had no doubt that was who they were—were striking back with a vengeance.

Suddenly a rifle boomed from the other side of the creek, then another. He ventured a look, saw one of the ambushers sag toward the edge only to be grabbed by a companion and jerked back. That rifle fire had had an effect, and it hadn't come from J. D., who was armed only with the revolver at the moment. Joe twisted his head to look behind him, and on the far side of the creek he saw the Hampton wagon, with

Ben and Nora crouched behind it, firing their rifles up toward the top of the canyon wall. They had heard the shooting and come back to help, Joe realized.

J. D. was still firing, too, although none of her shots since the first one had actually hit anything. But altogether, the shots from Joe, J. D., Hampton, and Nora were making things plenty hot for the bushwhackers. Suddenly, during a lull in the firing, Joe heard the pounding of hoofbeats up there and knew that at least some of the Hellhounds were pulling back. The shots from the rimrock died away.

Joe rolled out from under the wagon in time to see one last figure scurrying for safety. Another second and the man would be out of sight. Joe jerked up his pistol and squeezed off a shot, and the man's hat went flying. The man turned and fired the rifle he held one-handed, one last act of defiance before fleeing.

Joe felt something slap the outside of his left thigh with a white-hot touch, and then the whole leg went numb. It folded up underneath him, pitching him to the ground.

"Joe!" J. D. screamed when she saw him go down. Heedless of her own safety, she came out from behind the long tom and dashed out of the creek toward him, her sodden skirt tangling around her legs.

Ben and Nora Hampton sent a couple more shots at the top of the canyon wall, just to make sure the Hellhounds were gone, then got in their wagon and drove quickly across the creek to the camp. By the time they reached J. D. and Joe, J. D. was already kneeling beside her partner. Joe's denim pants, long since faded by the sun to an almost white, showed a bright blood stain on the left leg. J. D. looked up at Hampton and Nora and said unnecessarily, "Joe's been hit!"

"Should've . . . stayed where I was," Joe said between gritted teeth. "Damn fool stunt . . . coming out like that. Got what I . . . deserved."

"Hush!" J. D. told him. "You're going to be all right, Joe."

"Y-yeah. . . ." His fingers found hers, closed on them feebly. A gasp escaped from him, and then his eyes rolled up and his head fell back loosely.

"Joe!" J. D. screamed. "Oh, my God! Joe! You can't be dead, you just can't. . . ."

CHAPTER
11
....

Fury and Milo Phipps reached the camp just after dark that evening, and Fury knew something was wrong before they even got there. The fire was built up too big, and there were several wagons parked around the claim, as well as some extra saddle horses. Had the Hellhounds already moved back in and taken over everything? Fury held back until he saw a couple of figures he recognized in the firelight, Ben Hampton and Will Corey. Then he spurred forward quickly.

"What's wrong?" he called to Hampton and Corey as he entered the circle of light and reined in. "What's happened here?" Fury's pistol was out and held ready in his hand without him really being aware of it.

"There's been some trouble," Will Corey replied. "Your friend Brackett was shot—"

"Joe? Where is he?"

Ben Hampton held up both hands, palms out. "Take it easy, Mr. Fury. It's all over now, has been since early afternoon. That's when the Hellhounds ambushed your friends. But Joe's goin' to be all right, and Miz McKavett weren't hurt none at all."

Relief flooded through Fury. He holstered his gun and swung down from the saddle, motioning for Milo to do the same. He said, "I want to see Joe."

"He's in the tent," Hampton said. "Miz McKavett's tendin' to him. He got creased pretty good on the leg, lost quite a bit of blood. But it looked a heap worse'n it really was. I

113

cleaned it up with some whiskey, and if the wound don't fester, it ought to heal all right."

"You were here when it happened?" Fury asked.

"Nora and I brought some lunch over, and we'd just drove off when the Hellhounds jumped 'em. We came back and pitched in the fracas. Drove those bastards off pretty quick, but one of 'em got lucky as he was runnin' away. Threw one last shot at Joe, and it happened to hit him."

Fury put a hand on Hampton's shoulder and said fervently, "Thanks, Ben. Thanks for everything."

Hampton grinned. "Shoot, just bein' neighborly."

"Those murderers would have killed Brackett and Mrs. McKavett if Ben and his girl hadn't still been nearby," Corey said grimly. "We've got to do something about those Hellhounds. We've got to put a stop to this lawlessness." He gestured at the other men standing around the fire, all of whom were strangers to Fury. "These are most of the miners from the canyon. We're going to talk about banding together to wipe out the Hellhounds."

"Vigilance committee, eh?" Fury grunted. "Might not be a bad idea. You go ahead and have your meeting. I still want to see Joe."

"Come on," Hampton said. "We'll see if he's still awake."

"Wait out here, Milo," Fury told the youngster as Hampton started toward the tent. "I'll introduce you around later."

"Sure, Mr. Fury," Milo said with a nod.

Fury followed Hampton into the tent and saw Joe stretched out on a bedroll, his head propped up by a folded blanket that was serving as a pillow. J. D. sat beside him and held a cup of broth to his lips. She looked up at Fury and gave him a weak smile as Joe swallowed the last of the steaming liquid.

"Thank God you're back," she said.

"Heard you had trouble," Fury said as he knelt on the other side of Joe.

The young man gestured at his bandaged left thigh. "Don't worry about this," he declared. "Nothing but a little scratch."

"A little scratch that bled a great deal," J. D. said. "You just rest now, Joe."

"Not until he's told me exactly what happened."

J. D. looked squarely at Fury. "I'm perfectly capable of doing that. Joe needs some sleep. He's been through a lot today."

Joe wasn't the only one, Fury thought, remembering the landslide and Milo's near plunge down the cliff earlier in the day. But he kept that to himself and said to J. D., "All right, you tell me about it. Joe, you'd best do like the lady says and get some sleep."

"I *am* a mite tired," Joe admitted. He let his eyelids slide shut and settled his head back against the rolled-up blanket.

J. D. stood up and motioned for Fury to follow her as she left the tent. As they stepped outside, she said in a low voice, "He's going to be all right, I'm sure of it. I was really worried at first, but Mr. Hampton assured me the wound wasn't as bad as it looked."

"I'll take a look at it in the morning," Fury promised. "Those dressings'll need to be changed then anyway." He paused, then went on. "You said you'd tell me what happened . . . ?"

"It was awful," J. D. said with a shudder. "They were up on the canyon rim, shooting down at us. . . . I thought we were both going to die. We probably would have if Mr. Hampton and Nora hadn't come back to help us." Quickly, she gave Fury the details of the attack, then concluded by saying, "Joe was wounded right at the end of the fight. It was such bad luck. I wish I had gotten a shot at the man who hurt him."

"You were firing back at them, too?"

Ben Hampton came over to join them in time to hear Fury's question. "Firing at them?" he echoed. "Why, Miz McKavett knocked one o' them boys right off the rim, clean as you please. Joe told me about it while I was patchin' him up."

Fury looked at J. D., who had an uncomfortable expression on her face. "Is that true?" he asked.

"I shot one of them, yes. I'm sure it was luck as much as anything else."

Hampton jerked a thumb over his shoulder. "We got the body over there under a blanket. You can take a look at him if you want."

Fury nodded grimly and picked up a burning brand from the fire to illuminate the dead man's features. "Let's do that."

Hampton led the way over to the corpse, with Will Corey and some of the other men coming along, too. J. D. stayed behind, and Fury was glad of that. Thurl Hampton pulled back the corner of the blanket from the dead man's face. Fury studied the contorted features for a moment, then shook his head. "Bound to be one of the Hellhounds," he said, "but I don't recognize him. Thought it might be the one we ran off the other day."

One of the other men spoke up. "Oh, he's a Hellhound, all right. I seen him before, runnin' with that wild bunch over at that robbers' roost of theirs."

Fury glanced sharply at the man and said, "Robbers' roost? What are you talking about?"

"There's a place up in the northwest corner of the canyon, just under Cougar Bluff," Will Corey said, "where the gang is rumored to hide out. It's a roadhouse, I suppose you'd say, although the trail it's on couldn't be dignified by calling it an actual road."

Fury frowned. "You mean you know where to find these Hellhounds, and you haven't done anything about them before now?"

Ben Hampton grimaced and rubbed his beard-stubbled chin. "We ain't lawmen, Mr. Fury," he said. "Back where we come from, we were all farmers and store clerks and the like. We came out here to find gold, not to fight outlaws."

"The two things sometimes go hand in hand," Fury said.

"You're right," Corey said, his tone blunt and hard. "That's why I'm trying to organize a vigilance committee. We're never going to have any law and order around here until we do something about these criminals. Not just the organized gangs like the Hellhounds, but all the claim jumpers and thieves and low-down murderers who come out to the gold fields to take advantage of other people's hard work!"

Corey's voice was loud and ringing by the time he was through, and mutters of agreement came from the crowd of men. Fury could see how Corey might be able to mold them into a force that could deal with lawlessness. He had no idea what Corey had done before the man came out here to California, but obviously he possessed the ability to speak to people and move them.

"A vigilance committee might be a good idea," Fury said quietly. "But I favor a more direct approach."

"What do you mean, Mr. Fury?" Hampton asked.

"Let me think on it. In the meantime, Ben, do you think I could borrow one of your boys for a day or two?"

"Well, sure, I reckon," Hampton replied, looking confused. "What for?"

"After what happened here today, I don't much want to go very far from the claim again. But I've got a sack of out-going mail to be delivered to Alexander Todd's agent over in Sonora. I'd like for Dave or Thurl to carry it for me."

"I'd be glad to do that for you, Mr. Fury," Thurl said.

"There'll be some money in it for you," Fury added. "You'll be collecting the wages that are due me, too, so I can pay you. You'll be missing a day or two of work on your pa's claim."

"Whatever you think is fair, Mr. Fury," Hampton said. "Thurl can leave first thing in the morning, can't you, boy?"

"Sure, Pa."

Fury looked around at the circle of grim-faced men. "In the meantime, I want to know everything you can tell me about these bastards who call themselves the Hellhounds."

Mike Sullivan and Duncan Laidlaw were both still seething with anger, even though twenty-four hours had passed since the disastrous attack on the new claim in Last Chance Canyon. They had sent eight men over there, eight good men.

And those men had come back with their tails between their legs, chased off by an old man, a nigger, and two girls.

Seven of them had come back, anyway. The eighth had been left behind, shot down by one of those damn-blasted females.

It was enough to make a man sick to his stomach, Sullivan thought, as he swallowed the last of the beer in his bucket.

The two men were sitting at a table in the roadhouse that had been taken over for the unofficial headquarters of the Hellhounds. It was dim and hot in the barroom, but that was all right with Sullivan and Laidlaw. They were accustomed to life in the city, and they didn't have much use for the bright light of day.

Mike Sullivan was a burly, dark-eyed Irishman with black hair and a near-constant frown on his lantern-jawed face. He'd come to New York from the Ould Sod ten years earlier and immediately fallen in with a gang there. When it got too hot for him there, he had headed West, following the lure of gold like thousands of other men.

Sullivan had never intended to chip the gleaming stuff out of the rocks, or to pan the dust out of the rivers and creeks. Other men could do that, and then he would steal it once they brought it in to San Francisco. The whole thing was simple.

At least it had been until the vigilantes had smashed the gang known as the Hounds.

Laidlaw's story was similar. The grandson of a British convict who'd been shipped off to Australia, he had grown up in Sydney, learning many a valuable lesson at the knee of old Grandpap. Even across the wide Pacific, men in Australia had heard about the riches to be gained in California, and Laidlaw had joined the exodus to the gold fields. He had never gotten there, though, because his grandfather had asked him to look up an old friend in San Francisco, and as soon as Laidlaw had met the man, he had sensed a kindred spirit. Grandpap's friend was the leader of the Sydney Ducks, and young Duncan had become a part of the gang almost right away.

With a shock of ginger hair and a thick, drooping mustache that he had cultivated to make him look older, Laidlaw was a formidable figure. Tall and broad-shouldered, a seasoned brawler and a ruthless enemy, he had quickly worked his way up in the ranks of the Australian criminal organization.

And then the vigilance committees had run the Ducks out of town, too, after hanging several of them. Those untimely deaths left Laidlaw the leader of a gang with no place to operate.

It was fate that had brought Sullivan and Laidlaw together in a Hangtown tavern and given them the bright idea of merging their gangs. Both men were convinced of it, just as they were convinced it was their destiny to rule these gold fields with an iron hand.

Sooner or later, perhaps, their ambition would force a conflict between them as they fought it out for sole leadership of the organization. But until that day came, they were content to work together and grow rich.

Joe Brackett's claim was going to make them even richer, once they got their hands on it for good.

At the moment, Laidlaw's brain was working along the same lines as Sullivan's, and he said bitterly, "That feller Brackett's got to be the luckiest nigger alive. He ought to be dead, 'stead o' just creased."

"Aye," Sullivan agreed. "But we'll be gettin' 'im the next time, don't ya know?"

"Is there goin' to be a next time?"

"Of course there is," Sullivan declared belligerently. "I ain't lettin' a claim like that slip through me fingers." He turned around on the bench and shouted at the bartender, "Bring us some more beer over here, and be quick about it!"

"Sure, Mr. Sullivan," the bartender said. He was a medium-sized man with gray hair. He filled a couple of buckets from a huge keg, then carried them out to the table where Sullivan and Laidlaw sat.

The two gang leaders were the only customers at the moment, although one couldn't really call them customers since they never paid for what they drank. But they let the place keep on operating and only demanded half the profits, which the owner deemed a fair deal. If the Hellhounds wanted to, they could burn the roadhouse down or tear it into kindling. At least this way the proprietor made a little money from the few other customers who dared to come to the place these days. It sat on a formerly well-traveled trail, a sturdy log building at the base of a cliff with the huge shelf of rock known as Cougar Bluff jutting out above it.

There were cribs out back, and that was where the rest of the gang were, sleeping off the previous night's binge. They would be rolling out of bed soon, bleary-eyed and sick to their stomachs. Sullivan and Laidlaw had only been up a little while themselves, and the beer they were guzzling was their breakfast.

They spent the next few minutes drinking and cursing Joe Brackett and his companions. For several months now, the will of the Hellhounds had been law in these parts, and they could not allow their rule to be challenged, especially not by a black man. "Might as well let a bloody Chinaman tell us what to do," Laidlaw grumbled.

Sullivan nodded solemnly. "We may have to take charge of this ourselves, Duncan. That boyo's got to be killed. We got to make an example of him."

"Aye."

The back door of the roadhouse opened and three members of the gang stumbled in. They headed straight for the bar, and one of them croaked, "Whiskey!"

Sullivan grinned, and even that expression looked like a glare on his surly face. "Enoch sounds like he needs a mite o' the hair of the dog," he said.

The front door opened then, and since the three men who had just come in had neglected to shut the back door, a fresh spring breeze blew through the roadhouse, stirring the smoky, stale air. Light slanted in, and Sullivan winced as the glare struck him. "Shut that goddamn door!" he raged at the dimly seen figure standing there.

The man ignored the command. Instead, he said, "I'm looking for the Hellhounds."

"You found 'em, mate," one of the men at the bar growled. "What do you—Oh, hell! It's *him*!"

Laidlaw and Sullivan both started to their feet as the Australian barked, "Who?"

"The other bloke that was with the nigger—"

The man at the bar didn't say any more. He broke off his answer and clawed at the gun on his hip.

The pistol was only halfway out of its holster when the man in the doorway fired, the flare of his muzzle blast all but lost in the brilliant afternoon sunshine around him. Fury fired twice, both balls slamming into the chest of the man at the bar and driving him back against the planks laid atop barrels.

Fury pivoted smoothly and stepped out of the doorway at the same time, knowing he would be a target there, even if the men inside the gloomy barroom were half-blinded by the light. One of the other men at the bar had a gun out now and fired a wild shot at the fast-moving Fury. The bullet whipped past him, missing by a good two feet.

Fury saw that the two men were lined up just right and took advantage of the opportunity. He tipped up the barrel of the Sharps he carried in his left hand and squeezed the trigger. It was a daring, almost foolhardy, maneuver, and Fury knew it. But it worked. The recoil almost wrenched Fury's hand off, but the .50 caliber ball entered the belly of the first man, ripped through his vitals, then burst out his back still rising to catch the second man in the chest. The ball had lost enough of its momentum from hitting its first target that it didn't blow a fist-sized hole through the second man. Instead, the ball lodged in his heart and killed him anyway.

The two men hit the puncheons of the floor within a second of each other.

Fury ignored the pain in his left wrist and leveled the Dragoon at the two men at the table. The gunfight had taken only a handful of seconds, but it had seemed longer than that as the deafening roar of the blasts and the stench of burned powder and fresh blood filled the room. Laidlaw and Sullivan stood there and gaped at Fury, but they carefully kept their hands away from their guns.

The uproar would draw the rest of the Hellhounds on the run, Fury knew. He had only a moment now to deliver his message, but he had been lucky again. He recognized the two men at the table as Sullivan and Laidlaw, the leaders of the gang. Several men had described them the night before at the meeting of the miners, as well as giving him the location of this roadhouse.

"My name is John Fury," he said into silence that was all the more deafening for being preceded by the eruption of gunfire. "I'm Joe Brackett's friend, and I'm warning you to leave him and his claim alone. Seven of your men have died already, and more will unless you back off. The same holds true for the other claims." He moved his gaze back and forth between Sullivan and Laidlaw as he stared at them over the barrel of his Colt. "If you don't leave us alone, I'll kill you."

That was all that needed to be said.

Everything had happened so quickly that Laidlaw and Sullivan were still blinking a little from the unexpected brightness of the open door. They saw a flicker of movement there, and suddenly Fury was gone. Cursing furiously, Sullivan yanked his pistol out and ran toward the door.

Laidlaw caught up to him before he got there, grabbing Sullivan's shoulder and jerking him back. "He could still be out there, you bloody fool!" Laidlaw warned. "He might be just waitin' for you to stick that noggin of yours outside so's he can blow it off!"

"You're right," Sullivan said, trembling with rage. "But we can't just let him ride off!"

The sound of rapid hoofbeats came to their ears, and Laidlaw sighed. "I reckon that's about all we can do right now, mate."

More members of the gang suddenly spilled through the back door of the roadhouse, bristling with guns and ready to fight. "You're too damned late," Sullivan snarled at them. "He's already come in here and killed Ike and Enoch and Gus."

The other men looked at the bloody forms sprawled on the floor, and one of them asked, "Who the hell did this?"

"A man named John Fury," Laidlaw replied. "The nigger's friend." He added, "Soon to be a dead man."

"Can't be soon enough to suit me," Sullivan said. He put up his gun and turned to the bar, which had been half-destroyed by the dead man falling on it. The bartender was trying to pick up the planks and put them back on the barrels.

"Never mind that," Laidlaw said. "Bottles all around. Some of you men drag these bodies out and take care of them."

Sullivan didn't wait for the bartender to serve them. He reached over and took two bottles from one of the shelves on the back wall. He handed one to Laidlaw and said, "Here. I got a toast to make."

"I reckon I know what it is, too," Laidlaw said grimly.

Both men pulled the corks from the necks of the bottles and spat them out. The bottles clinked together.

Sullivan said, "To the death of John Fury."

"May he burn in hell," Laidlaw added.

They both drank to that.

CHAPTER
12

·····························

Fury's left wrist was still aching slightly as he rode up to the claim in Last Chance Canyon a little later. That had been a fool stunt, firing the Sharps one-handed; he had been lucky not to break his wrist. But it had worked out as the single shot killed two of the Hellhounds and stunned Laidlaw and Sullivan into not drawing on him.

If the Hellhounds' desire to move onto Joe's claim had been strong before, Fury's actions today would make it border on an obsession, and he knew it. He had made it personal by invading the gang's sanctum and gunning down three of them. That had been his plan. Sitting back and waiting for the Hellhounds to make the next move would have been too risky. Now he had them off balance and had served notice on them that the only way they'd get their hands on Joe's claim would be to pay a high price in men's lives. Maybe they would be reasonable and move on to easier pickings somewhere else.

Maybe—but Fury doubted it.

As he rode up, J. D. was shoveling dirt from the streambed into the long tom while Milo Phipps worked on the canyon wall with pick and shovel. Joe was seated on a good-sized rock with his wounded leg stretched out in front of him, a carbine across his lap and a shotgun on the ground beside him.

Fury reined in and grinned at him. "I didn't figure J. D. would even let you out of the tent today."

"I'm feeling a mite puny, all right," Joe admitted, "but not so bad that I can't sit out here and sort of supervise while I'm standing guard. Or sitting guard, in this case."

"Probably a good idea." Fury swung down from the saddle. "I had me a little talk with the leaders of the Hellhounds."

Joe's eyes widened in surprise. "What the hell? You just said you were going off on an errand, but I never figured it would be to go see the Hellhounds!"

J. D. and Milo had heard enough of the conversation to be interested, and they stopped their work long enough to come over and hear Fury's explanation. "I just went to that roadhouse where they spend most of their time and warned them to leave us alone," Fury said.

"And they stood for that?" J. D. asked.

"Well . . . three of them tried to shoot me."

"Any of them still alive?" Joe asked dryly.

"Not those three," Fury said with a shake of his head.

"Damn," Milo said softly. "And I was dumb enough to try to bushwhack you twice."

"Don't worry, Milo, you finally learned better," Fury told him. "Why don't you unsaddle my horse for me and stake him out with the others? I'll take that pick from you for a while."

"You sure about that, John?" Joe asked.

"A little honest work's not going to hurt me," Fury assured him. He took the pick from Milo and went over to the canyon wall. He could sense the others watching him as he lifted the tool above his head and then swung it in one smooth motion, the blade chipping into the rocky wall where Milo had been working. After a couple of minutes, when Fury glanced over his shoulder, he saw that J. D. had gone back to the long tom, Milo was taking care of the dun as Fury had requested, and Joe was keeping watch as before.

That afternoon set the tone for the next several days. Fury, Milo, and J. D. worked steadily, while Joe stood guard, recuperated from his wound, and complained about feeling guilty over the work the other three were doing on his claim. Fury and Milo alternated with the pick and shovel, and they also took turns spelling J. D. on the long tom. Some days they managed only a few hundred dollars' worth of gold, but on others—like the day Fury and Milo found a particularly rich vein in the canyon wall—they took several thousand dollars out of the claim. By the time a week had passed since Joe and J. D. had first started working, Fury estimated the claim had yielded almost ten thousand dollars' worth of nuggets and dust.

One afternoon, the Hampton wagon appeared again, with Nora Hampton at the reins. The redheaded young woman had another basket of food with her, and the group enjoyed the break from the routine they had been following, especially Milo, who spent quite a while talking to Nora. She seemed to be hanging on intently to his every word, and Fury had to hide a grin as he watched the two of them. Milo and Nora were hitting it off, and that was probably the best thing in the world that could have happened to the young man.

"Cute, aren't they?" J. D. asked in a quiet voice as she and Fury left the picnic lunch to get back to work.

"Who?"

"Milo and Nora. I saw you looking at them. Surely it's as obvious to you what's going on as it is to me."

"Well, yeah, I reckon it is," Fury said with a shrug. "It'll be a good thing for the boy, too. He needed some settling down, and Nora can do that."

"What about you?"

Fury frowned and shook his head. "I don't understand."

"Are you looking for the love of a good woman to settle *you* down?"

Fury didn't know whether to cuss or laugh. J. D. was prying into matters that didn't really concern her, but on the other hand, Fury had never been one to hide things about himself. Some folks said he was mysterious, but that was because they never really got to know him, what with all the gunplay that seemed to follow him around on his travels.

"I'm not looking to settle down," he told J. D. "With or without a good woman—or a bad one, for that matter."

She had the good grace to blush a little, but she had her teeth in the question now and wasn't going to let go. "Is that all you do, just drift around the West? No friends, no family, no place to come home to?"

"I've got friends," Fury protested, wondering why he was even wasting time arguing with this woman. "Joe and I have ridden together before." He looked squarely at her. "I'd like to think that you and me are friends, too."

That comment brought another flush to her face. "Yes, of course we are. But I'm talking about somebody who's more than a . . . a business associate, or someone to have at your side in a fight."

"Who's a better friend than that?" Fury asked pointedly.

J. D. sighed in exasperation. "You know what I mean, John. You're just being stubborn about it because you don't want to talk about it. You've built a wall around yourself, and you won't even let anyone peek over it."

Fury shook his head. "That's not true. I don't keep things to myself any more than anybody else does. Like you."

"Me?" J. D. said in surprise. "Why, I'm much more open than you!"

"Are you? Then how come I don't know how a pretty young woman like you came to be running a store all by herself in a place like San Francisco?"

"You never asked me," J. D. said, anger edging into her voice. "And as for that backhanded compliment, I suppose I should be grateful. I told you I was married. I also had a child. My husband and my son are both dead."

Suddenly Fury felt like a prize jackass. He had gotten impatient with J. D. for asking personal questions, so what had he done? Turned around and made matters worse by questioning *her* about things that were none of his business. He grimaced and muttered, "Sorry."

J. D. drew a deep breath and said, "That's all right. Perhaps I *should* tell you about it, so you'll understand why it's so important to me to make enough money from this venture to rebuild my store. You see, it's all I have left of my husband. It was his dream to be a successful merchant, and he's the one who built the store and got it started. We had a son, a darling little boy eight years old, and he was just beginning to help out around the place. Then . . . then the fever took them both." J. D. shook her head. "I've thought and thought, but I still don't understand why they were taken and I was spared. It was no kindness, I assure you. I'd rather have died with them."

She said the words quietly and simply, without any fuss or hysterics. But Fury never doubted for an instant her sincerity. He saw pain well up in her eyes at the memories he had roused, but then she forced it away and looked at him with an unreadable expression.

"I've done well in business, you know," she went on. "The store was thriving—until I decided to grubstake Joe and made myself an enemy of the Hellhounds in the process. But I don't hold that against him. It was my choice to throw in with him, as you'd say."

"If I've caused you any hurt, I'm sorry," Fury told her. "I didn't mean to. Reckon I ought to be as honest with you as you were with me and tell you how I came to be so fiddle-footed—"

J. D. was shaking her head. "That's not necessary. In fact, I believe I'd rather not know. Let's just . . . go on about our business, shall we? We have gold to find."

For a few seconds, Fury didn't say anything. Then he nodded. "That's right. There's gold to find." He hefted the pick. "And I'm going to get back to it."

J. D. went on to the long tom while Fury returned to the canyon wall. As he chipped away at the rock, he thought about the tragic story J. D. had just told him. He had known some tragedies of his own in the past, but he had put them behind him and made a life for himself, even if it did involve a lot of drifting and stumbling into trouble. In her own way, J. D. had done the same thing. The two of them were a lot alike, even though J. D. probably wouldn't admit to such a thing.

A little grin played around Fury's mouth, and he drove the pick into the rock wall again.

"I really ought to be getting back to work," Milo told Nora. "Ain't right letting Mr. Fury and Miz McKavett handle everything."

"I'm sure they wouldn't mind if you talked to me just a few minutes longer," Nora said quickly.

"Well . . . I reckon not."

"You were telling me about the farm you and your brother had back East," Nora prompted.

Milo nodded. "It never amounted to much. Belonged to our pa, it did, and after he passed on, Johnny and me never thought about doing anything else except staying there and trying to make a go of it. Our ma died when we were just little sprouts, and neither one of us hardly even remembered her. Working on that farm was all we knew. Then Johnny happened to look at an old newspaper once in town whilst he was picking up supplies."

With his voice taking on a new air of excitement, Milo went on. "There was a story in that paper about gold out here in California. Told how there was so much gold you couldn't hardly walk for tripping over great big nuggets worth thousands of dollars." He shook his head. "Maybe it was that way once, but it sure ain't now. More than likely the fella who wrote that just didn't know his . . . Well, didn't know what he was talking about, let's say."

"I don't recall Pa or the boys stumbling over any great big nuggets, either," Nora said. "All the gold they've found, they've worked for."

"That's probably what all of you expected when you came out here, though. Johnny and me, we figured we'd get rich right away. Thought we'd pick up gold from the ground for a month or so and then go back home and never have to work again." Milo shook his head sadly. "Sure didn't work out that way."

"You never found *any* gold?"

"Nary a bit. We tried digging, panning, everything we could think of. Never even a speck of color. I wanted to give up, but Johnny was stubborn. He stuck with it, even after I'd gotten that job carrying the mail for Mr. Todd." There was a catch in Milo's voice as he went on. "Johnny was still trying to find gold, right up until the time he took over that mail run for me 'cause I was sick. And that was the death of him."

Nora put a hand on his arm and said softly, "You don't have to tell me about that if you don't want to. I know it must be mighty painful for you."

"No, I want you to know about it." In a halting voice, Milo repeated the story Fury had told him about his brother's death and the aftermath of the holdup that had taken Johnny's life. He continued, "For a while, I was crazy mad with grief, I reckon. I got it twisted around in my head that Mr. Fury was responsible for Johnny dying. So I tried to bushwhack him and even the score—not once, but twice. Like to got *myself* killed the second time."

"I'm sorry, Milo," Nora told him. "I'm sorry about your brother and about all the trouble you've had. You deserve better."

"I don't know if I do or not," Milo said with a shake of his head. "I was plenty dumb, and I'm not just talking about blaming Mr. Fury. All the way back to when Johnny and me decided to come out here, I ain't been very smart. Nor lucky. I'm a walking Jonah, Nora, and I reckon you're taking a chance just sitting here with me."

She smiled a little and looked down toward the ground. "I'll take that chance," she said shyly.

Milo felt a warm tightness in his chest, sort of like that time he'd eaten too many Mexican peppers but a whole lot better. It was uncomfortable but mighty nice at the same time.

"Things are going to be different now," he said, his voice full of unaccustomed determination. "Mr. Fury spoke up for me and convinced Joe and Miz McKavett to give me a chance, and I don't intend to let any of them down. I'll do my best to help 'em, and Joe says I can have a share in the claim in return if I do good. I'll have enough money to buy another farm, this time a good one that I can really make something out of."

"I believe you, Milo." Nora reached over and took hold of his hand, squeezing his fingers. "I really believe you. I . . . I'd sure like to go back to a nice farm someday myself."

That warm feeling inside him was getting hotter and more uncomfortable than ever. Swallowing hard, he began, "Maybe we could—"

When he didn't go on, Nora asked, "Maybe we could what, Milo?"

He shook his head. "Nothing," he said. "It wasn't nothing."

He had come mighty close to asking her if she'd go to the new farm with him, as his wife. But that was crazy, Milo told himself. He hardly knew this girl, and she sure as hell didn't know him! She didn't know how he'd toted bad luck around with him wherever he went and how it rubbed off on those he cared about. Just look at what had happened to Johnny. . . .

"Milo," Nora said firmly, cutting into his gloomy thoughts, "anytime you want to say something to me, you just go ahead and say it. There's nothing you can say or do that'll make me think any less of you."

She just didn't know, Milo thought. Didn't have any idea.

He might have tried to explain, might have told her that the smartest thing for her to do would be to steer well clear of a jinx like him, but he never got around to it. The sound of hoofbeats made him look up, and the same noise alerted Joe, J. D., and Fury.

Somebody was coming, and from the way they were riding fast across the canyon, they weren't bringing good news.

CHAPTER
13
·····························

Fury laid down his pick and hurried over to the tent to pick up the Sharps. Joe was already on his feet, standing with his weight on the uninjured leg. Milo and Nora came over from where they had been sitting beside the Hampton wagon, and J. D. joined them, leaving her shovel lying on the creekbank beside the long tom.

From the sound of the hoofbeats, there was only one rider approaching, and Fury doubted that any of the Hellhounds would attack them single-handedly. Still, he wanted to be ready in case of trouble.

The horseman came into view, and when Fury recognized Will Corey's tall, powerful form, he relaxed slightly. But only slightly, because from the way Corey was whipping his horse into a lather, something was mighty wrong.

Corey splashed across the creek and reined in with a shout to his horse. Sounding a little breathless, he said to the five people near the tent, "Howdy, folks. Hope I didn't startle you by galloping up like this. But I've got news, bad news."

"Figured as much," Joe said. "What is it, Mr. Corey?"

"Old Ansel Davis across the canyon has been killed," Corey said bluntly. "He was robbed and murdered last night."

"Mr. Davis?" Nora exclaimed. "Oh, no!"

"Don't reckon we knew the man," Joe said, "but we're sorry to hear about it anyway."

"He was an old-timer, one of the first men to stake a claim in the canyon," Nora explained. "He was always friendly to Pa and the boys and me. You say he was robbed, Mr. Corey?"

Corey nodded grimly. "That's right. The old man never dug much gold out of that ground of his, but I know he had a small poke. He was going to send it in to the bank in San Francisco as soon as he got a chance. But it's gone now." Corey's face flushed with righteous anger as he went on. "I rode over to his claim a little while ago to tell him about the vigilance committee meeting tonight, and I found him outside his tent with his head stove in. Looked like somebody had hit him with a rock or a length of firewood."

"Dear Lord," J. D. breathed.

"His gear had been gone through, of course, and his poke was gone."

"Any sign of who might've done it?" Fury asked.

"I found a few tracks," Corey said. "You have to understand, I'm not very good at reading sign. Never picked up the knack of it. But from what I could tell, the tracks led north—straight toward the claim of those Jeffords boys."

Fury shook his head, not knowing who Corey was talking about, and again Nora supplied the explanation. "Tom and Hobie and Pete Jeffords. They've got a claim not far from ours. But they're no-accounts. Pa says they're not really willing to work, that they just wanted to get rich quick." She flushed a little. "They used to call out rude things to me every time I'd ride by their place by myself, until Thurl and Dave went over there and whipped 'em. Now they leave me alone."

"Wish I'd been around then," Milo said angrily. "I'd have helped your brothers thrash those boys."

Fury didn't particularly care what the Jeffords brothers had done in the past. He asked Corey, "You reckon they'd stoop to killing an old man and stealing his gold?"

"I think they would," Corey said with a sigh. "I'm riding around the canyon now, rounding up men so that we can go see about this. I planned to have a meeting tonight anyway, as I mentioned, but I didn't have any idea we'd have a cowardly murder to avenge."

"I'll go with you," Fury said. "I remember Davis now from that first meeting. Didn't seem the type to do any harm to anybody."

"He wasn't," Corey agreed.

Joe said, "This leg of mine's healed up enough so that I can go with you."

"I'm in, too," Milo said.

Fury shook his head at both of them. "You'd better stay here and keep an eye on the claim. The Hellhounds'd like nothing better than if we all went off and left J. D. here by herself."

"I can go with the vigilance committee," J. D. suggested.

Corey tugged his hat off and said quickly, "Begging your pardon, Mrs. McKavett, but I don't think a lady of your breeding should be involved in any vigilante actions. It just wouldn't be seemly, ma'am."

"Well . . . perhaps you're right," J. D. agreed reluctantly. "I'll stay here."

"And so will the rest of you," Fury grunted. "Corey and me and a few of the other men can handle this." He headed for the makeshift corral where the horses were staked out, intending to saddle the dun.

Corey walked his horse along beside Fury. In a low voice, he said, "Thanks for offering to come along, Mr. Fury. I know you've had some, ah, experience in matters like these, and I'm sure your assistance will be welcome."

"If those Jeffords boys put up a fight and there's gunplay, you mean." Fury's voice was flat and hard.

"That's exactly what I mean, and I'm not going to apologize for it. We have to use whatever methods are required to bring at least some vestiges of law and order to this canyon."

Fury didn't argue with that sentiment. He just saddled up and rode out of the camp with Corey.

During the next hour, the two men visited several other claims, including Ben Hampton's, and the reaction they got at each one to the news of Ansel Davis's murder was the same: anger, outrage, and a vow that something had to be done. At the end of that hour, a force of over a dozen men was riding toward the piece of rocky ground claimed by the three Jeffords brothers. Thurl and Orville Hampton had been sent to Davis's claim to dig a grave for the murdered man.

If Tom, Hobie, and Pete Jeffords were responsible for the old man's killing, it was possible that they had already lit out, leaving the canyon behind them. If that was the case, Fury felt fairly certain he could track them, but he wasn't sure how many of the vigilantes would be willing to go with him and leave their claims unprotected behind them. He couldn't blame them if they turned around and went home. On the other hand, maybe the killers had felt confident enough that they hadn't fled.

It didn't take long to reach the Jeffords claim, and the noise made by the approaching group of riders must have warned the three brothers. As the vigilantes reached the edge of the claim, Tom, Hobie, and Pete stepped out of their ramshackle hut, each of them holding a rifle.

"Better stop right there!" one of them called out. Fury didn't know which one he was. All of them looked pretty much the same, scraggly sorts with dirty blond beards and patched clothes. "What are you gents doin' here?"

"I think you know perfectly well why we're here, Jeffords," Corey said, his voice full of anger. "You and your brothers killed Ansel Davis this morning."

"What? You mean to say that ol' coyote's dead?"

Fury could hear the insincerity in the startled exclamation and knew right away that the man was lying when he tried to act like Davis's murder was a surprise. All three of the Jeffords brothers were guilty as hell, and every man in the impromptu posse knew it.

"There's no point in putting on an act," Corey went on. "We've come to bring you men to justice. You killed a harmless old-timer and stole his meager goods, and you have to pay the price for that, damn it!"

"You got no proof!" one of the brothers protested. "We been here all mornin'. Ain't that right, fellers?"

The other two nodded vehemently.

One of the vigilantes cried, "You ain't goin' to believe those sorry bastards, are you, Will? They're lyin', and we can all see it!"

"Yeah!" another man agreed. "Let's string up the sons o' bitches!"

Fury had been sitting quietly during the confrontation, his hands crossed on the saddle horn. Now he spoke up, his voice not loud but possessing enough of an edge to cut through the angry hubbub.

"If they stole the old man's poke," he said, "the gold's probably hidden in their cabin. It's not a very big place, so I reckon a search would turn up the loot."

The Jeffords brothers started to lift their rifles. "Nobody's searchin' our cabin!" one of them yelled.

Fury had hoped to avoid gunplay, but he saw now it wasn't going to be possible. His hand went to his Colt as one of the brothers fired without aiming toward the group of vigilantes.

In the next split second, Fury fired, the ball from his revolver ripping through the upper arm of the second brother. Those were single-shot rifles they were carrying, so with that first wild shot, one of the brothers had rendered himself pretty much harmless. Fury's shot disarmed the second one. The man howled in pain, dropped his gun, and staggered back clutching his suddenly bloody arm. Fury switched his aim as he thumbed back the hammer for another shot, and he saw the eyes of the third Jeffords brother widen in fear as he stared at the man over the Dragoon's sights.

"Don't shoot!" the third brother yelped as he dropped his rifle and thrust his hands into the air in surrender.

The exchange of shots had happened so fast that none of the other vigilantes had had a chance to pull trigger. Now that the Jeffords had had their fangs pulled, several men spurred forward, dropped from their saddles, and grabbed the brothers.

"We gonna string 'em up, Will?" one of them asked Corey.

"Not until we've searched their cabin," Corey said. "We all know they're guilty, but we're going to do this legal-like."

There was a disappointed mutter from the committee. "You don't mean we're goin' to waste a lot of time takin' these no-good bastards back to Frisco to turn 'em over to the law, do you?" one of the miners wanted to know.

Corey shook his head. "I certainly don't. But they're entitled to a trial—after which, we'll dispense our own brand of justice."

That statement brought a cheer of approval from the men.

Fury holstered his Colt. The shooting was over.

All that was really left now was the hanging.

Fury's features settled into a grim mask. He had roamed the West enough to know that many times it just wasn't practical for every crime to be judged in a real court. On the frontier, folks usually had to take the law into their own hands if there was to be any law at all. But even while he acknowledged the necessity for lynch-rope justice, it was still an unpleasant business.

He swung down from the saddle and followed Corey into the brothers' cabin. It wasn't that he didn't trust Corey, but Fury had come this far and wanted to see the matter through to its conclusion.

It took them only a few minutes to find the small leather pouch full of tiny nuggets. The shack had a plank floor instead of the usual dirt, and several of the boards were loose. The pouch was underneath one of them, and when Corey found it and lifted it into the air for Fury's inspection, the letters "A. D." were plain to see, burned into the leather in a crude fashion.

"I've seen old Ansel with this pouch more than once," Corey said. "It's his poke, all right."

"Reckon we'd better go tell the others," Fury said. He knew what their reaction to this discovery would be.

As expected, a fresh howl went up from the vigilantes at the sight of the old man's poke. The Jeffords brothers weren't even bothering to deny anything anymore. They stood in surly silence, except for the wounded man, who let out an occasional whimper of pain.

A grim-faced Will Corey pointed out six members of the group and said, "You men are our jury, and as the mayor of Last Chance Canyon, I hereby declare that this miners' court is in session. Tom, Hobie, and Pete Jeffords stand accused of murder and robbery in connection with the death of Ansel Davis." He held up the pouch full of nuggets again and went on. "You've all seen this poke that belonged to Davis, and you know it was found inside the cabin belonging to the Jeffords brothers."

Fury could tell that the crowd was getting impatient, but Corey wasn't through yet. He was determined to do this right.

Turning his gaze to the prisoners, Corey asked, "Do you boys have anything to say in your own behalf before the jury decides your guilt or innocence?"

"This ain't no real trial," one of the brothers spat. "You and all the rest of these bastards can go to hell, Corey!"

"All right." Corey turned back to the men he had selected as the jury. "What's your verdict, gentlemen?"

"Guilty as sin!" shouted one of the jury members, and the others echoed his angry response.

"And the punishment for their crime?"

"Hang 'em!"

It was a foregone conclusion, of course, and Fury didn't see any reason to put a stop to things. Anybody who would stove in a harmless old man's head with a rock didn't deserve to live, not in a civilized community, anyway.

But there was still something bothering him about this. Maybe it was the sanctimonious look on Corey's face as the mayor turned to the prisoners and said, "You boys heard the sentence. Got anything to say now?"

"I said it before, and I'll say it again—go to hell!"

Corey waved a hand. "Let's get to it."

There was only one suitable tree in the vicinity, and the vigilantes shoved the prisoners toward it, whooping and shouting the whole way. Fury stepped up into his saddle and watched from horseback, staying where he was. It was going to be an ugly sight, and he knew it. Instead of putting the Jeffords brothers up on horses and arranging a quick, short drop that would break their necks, their hands were tied behind their backs, nooses were dropped around their throats, and they were hauled up, kicking and thrashing, to slowly strangle. There were no more chances for last words, no ceremony to the thing at all. Just harsh, brutal frontier justice.

As the faces of the Jeffords brothers turned blue and purple and their tongues began to protrude grotesquely, as they voided themselves with a horrible stench, as their frantic struggles grew more and more feeble, some of the vigilantes turned away, their faces twisted with sickness and revulsion. The lynching frenzy was over, and now these men would live with the memory of what they had done burned into their brains. Will Corey didn't turn away, though, Fury noticed, until the whole thing was over and the bodies were swaying loosely in the shade of the tree.

Ben Hampton walked over to where Fury sat on the dun. Hampton's face was pale and drawn, and he was rubbing his jaw and grimacing. "Lordy," he said in a hushed voice. "I ain't goin' to waste any sympathy on those skunks, but Lordy! That was a horrible thing to see."

"Yes, it was," Fury agreed. "Those three won't murder any more old men, though."

"Yeah, there's that. Still, I could've done without watchin' it."

"One of the prices we pay for justice," Fury said. He turned his horse. "Come on."

The mob broke up quickly, most of the men heading back to their own claims. Fury didn't know if Corey was going to cut down the bodies and have them buried, or leave them there as a lesson to anybody else who might be thinking of turning outlaw. At the moment, he didn't particularly care, either.

Ben and Dave Hampton rode part of the way with Fury, then veered off toward their own holdings. Fury headed back to Joe's claim, and when he got there, he found Joe and J. D. working together at the long tom.

"Where's Milo?" Fury asked as he dismounted.

"He took Nora back over to the Hampton place," Joe replied. "What happened, John?"

Fury shrugged. "We found the men who robbed and killed the old-timer. It wasn't hard. Like most men who do things like that, they weren't very smart."

"They put up a fight?"

"A little bit of one. Then they surrendered, and Corey had a trial for 'em."

"What was the verdict?" J. D. asked.

Fury and Joe looked at each other. Both of them knew the answer to that question, and Joe wouldn't have even bothered asking it. Fury said quietly, "The vigilantes hung all three of them."

"That . . . that's terrible!" J. D. took a deep breath. "But I suppose it had to be done."

"Corey thought so," Fury said curtly. He started unsaddling the dun.

"What do you mean by that?" J. D. demanded. "You don't think Will should have let those men go, do you?"

"Nope. They killed the old man, there's no doubt about that, so they got what was coming to them." Fury hesitated. "But I didn't much care for the look on Corey's face while they were dancing on the end of their ropes. I reckon he got a taste of power today . . . and he liked it."

"That's a horrible thing to say!" J. D. cried, throwing down her shovel. "You make it sound like Will enjoyed hanging those men. I'm sure he didn't, but he still thought it was necessary."

Fury just shrugged.

J. D. caught his arm. "You're jealous of Will, aren't you?"

The accusation took Fury totally by surprise. "Jealous? Of Corey? What in hell for?"

"Because . . . because I think he's such an interesting man." J. D.'s chin came up defiantly. "Because he's an educated man. He was a teacher before he came out here, you know."

Fury shook his head. "No, I didn't know that."

"Well, he was. He taught at a very prestigious academy in Vermont."

"Told you that during one of your conversations, did he?"

"As a matter of fact, he did."

"Well, that's fine." Fury turned away. Over his shoulder, he added, "I don't really care where the gent came from or what he did there. All I said was that he seemed mighty fond of the power of life and death."

J. D.'s voice lashed at him. "And isn't that exactly what you carry in that holster of yours, Mr. Fury?"

He stiffened, unsure how to answer her. The worst part about it was that she was right. For more years than he liked to think about, the Colt on his hip had indeed represented the power of life and death.

"We've got work to do," he finally said, and he strode away without looking back.

CHAPTER
14
....

John Fury could be an absolutely insufferable man, but J. D. told herself sternly that she had dealt with such men before. After all, she had made a success out of the store back in San Francisco, and to do that she'd had to overcome the natural resistance most men felt in dealing with a businesswoman. She would go on about the work she had to do, and Fury could go jump into a ravine for all she cared.

Which was one reason she was so surprised a week after the incident with the vigilantes when Nora Hampton came to her for advice on what to do about Milo.

"I swear, he's as stubborn as a mule, Miz McKavett," Nora said to her as the two women knelt beside the creek, out of easy earshot of the men. They were washing clothes in the icy water, and while J. D. didn't enjoy the chore, at least it was something different from the tedious job of shoveling dirt into the long tom. Milo was doing that at the moment, and Nora's eyes kept straying to his tall, slender figure some fifty yards down stream.

"What makes you say that, Nora?" J. D. asked, not really wanting to get involved in the young woman's problems but unwilling to turn her away. Nora had been very helpful around the camp, coming over nearly every day to take care of some chore or other for them. Of course, she was really coming to see Milo, J. D. thought, but that was all right.

"I know he loves me, Miz McKavett. I'm just sure of it. And he's started to tell me so a couple of times. But he always stops just before he gets around to it, and then he's like an ol' mule. You can't budge him."

"I've seen the way Milo looks at you," J. D. replied gently, "and for what it's worth, I think he loves you, too. But I know you'd like to hear him say it."

"Durn right. He talks about buying a farm somewhere, too, and I've told him how much I'd like to have a little place of my own. I've all but picked up a piece of firewood and whopped him over the head with it, Miz McKavett! If he'd just ask me to marry him, I'd say yes in a minute."

"Milo seems to be a fine young man," J. D. said as she scrubbed a shirt in the frigid stream. "I had my doubts at first when Mr. Fury brought him back to the claim. . . . After all, Milo *had* taken a few shots at us in the past. . . . But it's worked out just fine. He's a hard worker, and he seems devoted to Mr. Fury now."

"If he just didn't have a head as thick as that cliff over there," Nora muttered.

The young woman had not been the only visitor to the camp. Will Corey had been there, too. In fact, Corey had been spending so much time around the camp that Fury had started asking pointed questions about when the mayor worked on his own claim.

J. D. didn't care. She enjoyed Will's company. As she had told Fury, he was an educated man, and he could talk about more things than gold mining. He had read books and seen plays and knew more about more things than any man J. D. had run into out here on the frontier. She was always glad to see him riding up.

Of course, Fury, Joe, and Milo might think she was neglecting her share of the work in order to visit with Corey, but J. D. didn't believe that was fair. The amount of gold dust they were taking out of the stream was steadily diminishing, but the veins they had found in the canyon wall had become richer and richer. The piddling amount of dust she might miss by talking to Corey wasn't really worth worrying about, she told herself.

"Miz McKavett?"

Nora's voice broke into J. D.'s thoughts. She smiled at the girl and said, "I'm sorry. I suppose I let my mind drift away for a moment there. What were you saying?"

"I was just asking if you thought I ought to tell Milo that I love him."

J. D. frowned and considered the problem. "He might think you were rather forward if you did that," she finally said. "But it may come to that eventually. I believe I'd give him a little more time if I were you. You can't ever tell, he may still come around on his own."

Nora sighed. "I sure hope so. I'm gettin' mighty tired of waiting for some damn fool man to make up his mind."

J. D. had to laugh. "You and nearly every other woman in the world, Nora," she said.

Somebody raided Ben Hampton's claim three nights later, shooting up the cabin, busting Ben's picks and shovels, and caving in the shaft he and his boys had sunk into the side of the canyon. When the small keg of black powder they threw into the shaft went off, the blast shook the whole canyon. It was a miracle none of the Hamptons were badly hurt; they escaped the raid with only a couple of bullet burns.

"It was the damned Hellhounds, I know it!" Hampton declared when the other miners came to see what was going on. "They're tryin' to run me off so's they can jump my claim! But we'll just see about that! The boys and me ain't budgin'!"

Fury looked over at Will Corey, who was frowning in the light from a torch. "What about it, Corey?" Fury asked. "Are the vigilantes riding against the Hellhounds?"

"There's no proof, damn it!" Corey burst out reluctantly. "You heard Ben yourself, Fury. He and his boys and Nora never got a good look at the raiders."

"Well, who else could it've been but the Hellhounds?" Hampton demanded.

"I agree with you, Ben," Corey said, his voice soothing. "But we can't do anything without proof, or we'll be outlaws just as much as they are. When we hung the Jeffords boys, we had that poke of old Ansel's as evidence. That made it legal."

"The authorities in San Francisco might not think so," Fury pointed out. "We still took the law into our own hands."

Corey flushed angrily. "Not as far as I'm concerned. We're going to have law and order here in Last Chance Canyon, but we're going to do it the right way, blast it! And starting a war with the Hellhounds when we don't have any proof they're behind this outrage isn't the right way."

There was a lot of dissatisfied muttering, but the group of miners couldn't work up enough determination to go against Corey's wishes. Fury knew he could probably have roused them to action with a few well-chosen words, but that would have pitted him against Corey for leadership of the canyon's law-abiding population. He wasn't willing to go that far . . . not yet, anyway.

Besides, Corey could be right. There were other cutthroats and outlaws in the Sierra Nevadas besides the Hellhounds. It could have been a drifting gang of desperadoes that had attacked the Hampton claim.

Not likely . . . but possible.

The miners headed back to their own claims, and before he rode off, Fury said to Hampton, "Keep your eyes open, Ben. I've got a feeling things are going to get worse around here before they get better."

Hampton sighed. "I'm afraid you're right, John."

Another few days passed. The color in the stream next to Joe's claim had just about played out, but Fury, Joe, and Milo were still taking placer gold out of the canyon wall in impressive chunks. Joe's wounded leg had healed by now, and he was doing his full share of the work again. Most of the time, he and Fury and Milo were all working with picks and shovels, while J. D. stood guard armed with a six-gun and rifle. She had all but abandoned the long tom, since the amount of dust that the long tom was collecting wasn't really worth the effort it took to get it.

Corey hadn't shown up as much the past couple of days, and Fury wondered if it was because of the growing hostility between the two of them. He was sure J. D. believed that he was jealous of Corey because he was interested in her himself. That wasn't true—Fury liked and admired J. D. McKavett for the way she had risen above the adversity that had plagued her life, but he wasn't in love with her. J. D. probably wouldn't accept that, though, not when she had it in her head that Fury and Will Corey were both attracted to her.

One day when Corey came to the camp, he was riding hard again. "Trouble," he explained tersely when he had reined in. "A couple of miners down in the south end of the canyon were robbed early this morning, just before dawn. Four men burst into their cabin, shot them, and took their gold. One of the miners was killed in the attack, but the other lived long enough to reach a neighboring claim and spread the news before he died. I'm gathering volunteers to ride after the killers."

"I'll come along," Fury said. "What about you, Joe?"

"Think I'd rather stay and keep an eye on the place," Joe said. "No offense, Corey, but I'm not much inclined to join a bunch of vigilantes. Saw too many lynchings back where I came from."

"Yes, I rather imagine you did," Corey said. "What about you, Phipps?"

"I'll ride with you," Milo replied. "If Joe and Mr. Fury think it's all right."

"Sure, Milo," Joe told him. "You go ahead. J. D. and I can take care of the claim."

Fury had seen J. D. practicing with both rifle and pistol, and he agreed with Joe's assessment. J. D. had turned into a fine shot, and as long as she kept her head, she would make a good ally in case of trouble.

"Let's go," Fury said, heading for the corral to get his horse.

The vigilantes were more organized this time. Corey had sent men out to other sections of the canyon to gather reinforcements, and the posse converged in the center of the canyon. Once they were all together, they rode north, pushing their mounts hard as they tried to catch up to the marauders.

Fury had a hunch the men responsible for the deaths of the miners were not members of the Hellhounds, and that suspicion was confirmed late that afternoon when the vigilantes caught up with the fugitives, north of the canyon itself in some rugged foothills. There was a short but fierce gun battle as the thieves turned and tried to fight it out with their pursuers, but after two of them had been shot out of their saddles—Milo Phipps accounting for one of them—the two survivors surrendered.

Fury and all the other vigilantes knew what was going to happen next. The thieves still had the loot on them, stowed in their saddlebags. It didn't matter which six men Corey selected to serve as a jury; the verdict would have been the same no matter who was deciding it.

When the trial was over and the two prisoners were dangling lifelessly from the branch of a tree, the vigilantes turned and rode back home. Fury noticed that not quite as many of them looked upset at the sight of the lynching this time.

Hanging men was like anything else. It got easier the more you did it.

The sun was beating down from overhead. Spring had almost turned to summer, and even though the nights were still chilly up here in the mountains, the days were downright hot. Fury and Milo were chipping hunks of rock away from the canyon wall, and Joe was loading the cart and trundling it over to the spot where he inspected the ore for nuggets.

They had carved a sizable hunk off the side of the cliff in the two months they had been here, Fury thought. And there was over fifty thousand dollars worth of gold in the tent to show for their efforts. Fury had already started thinking about the best way to go about getting the gold into town. With the way lawlessness was on the rise around here again, it wouldn't be safe for one man to transport the gold to San

Francisco. He thought he'd check with Ben Hampton and some of the other miners, maybe get together a well-armed group of men to take everybody's nuggets and dust down out of the mountains, while leaving behind enough men to continue guarding the claims. Such cooperative efforts had worked well in other places, and Fury was sure they would here, too.

Suddenly, the sound of Fury's pick hitting the rock wall took on a different tone. He frowned, drew back the pick, and struck again. The noise didn't have the same ring to it that steel striking quartz did. He looked intently at the cliff face, then said in a low, intense voice, "Joe, Milo, come here a minute."

Both men came over to join him, and Joe asked, "What is it, John?"

Fury pointed at the wall. "Look," he said.

After a moment, Joe let out a low whistle. Milo gaped at Fury's discovery and then asked, "Is that *pure* gold?"

"I think so," Fury said. "The question now is, how far does the ledge extend?"

As if that was a signal, all three men began attacking the canyon wall with their picks, chipping away at the stone that still concealed most of the discovery Fury had uncovered. Fury's pulse was pounding wildly in his head. He was no more immune to the lure of gold fever than any other man.

And he could already tell this was one hell of a lode.

J. D. sensed their excitement and hurried over, and it was all she could do not to grab a pick and start using it herself. More and more of the rock was knocked away, and after a few hectic minutes, J. D. asked in a quavering voice, "Just how big *is* it?"

They had already uncovered an area extending several feet in each direction, and there was no sign of the end of the vein, just as there was no way of knowing how deep into the wall it went. The section they could already see would be worth tens of thousands of dollars once they had pried it out of the cliff.

"Wait a minute," Fury finally said. "Hang on, blast it! There's no point in killing ourselves like this. That rock's not going anywhere."

"You're right," Joe said grudgingly. "I'd sure like to know just how big that ledge is, though. We really are rich now. You'll be able to build the finest store in San Francisco, J. D. Hell, the finest one west of the Mississippi! And Milo, you can start plowing that farm of yours anytime you're ready." He looked over at Fury. "What about you, John?"

"I just came along to give you a hand, Joe, not for a stake in the claim."

"What?" Joe exclaimed. "That's not fair! You've done more than anybody—"

"Oh, I'll take some of the money, don't worry about that," Fury told him. "But I didn't sign on to become some sort of gold tycoon. All I need's enough to outfit me for a while."

"We'll argue about it later," Joe said as he leaned on his pick. "Right now, I've just about caught my breath, so I want to get back to work on this magnificent chunk of rock!"

Fury just grinned.

Joe deserved all his good fortune, as did J. D. and Milo. They had all worked hard, damned hard, for this find. Fury was glad for all three of them.

After they had worked a while longer, Fury said, "We could use some blasting powder. That rock around the ledge is getting more stubborn."

Joe wiped sweat from his face. "You're right. Some powder'd make things go quicker. But we're out of it. Used the last of it on that outcrop over yonder a couple of days ago."

"I'll bet Ben Hampton's got some," Milo suggested. "I know he sent for some after those raiders collapsed his shaft. He had to blast out some of the rubble before him and his boys could get in there to set things right. Nora told me." He blushed a little as he revealed the source of his information.

"Reckon you'd mind going over there and seeing if they'd sell us some of it?" Fury asked.

Milo's quick grin was just what Fury expected. Not only would the blasting powder help them uncover this rich vein, but he'd also have a chance to see Nora. "Sure, I'll go," he said without hesitation. "I'll just put on a clean shirt. . . ."

A few minutes later, as Milo rode off toward the other side of the canyon, Fury commented, "There goes a boy in love."

J. D. laughed. "And what would you know about that, John?"

"You might be surprised."

"I doubt it," J. D. said haughtily.

Joe pointed at the canyon wall. "I'm going back to work, if anybody cares to join me."

"Sure," Fury said. "No point in arguing. Some things are just too stubborn to be budged without blasting powder, like that rock."

J. D. just glared at him, crossed her arms, and didn't say anything else. After a moment, though, she started smiling again. She couldn't help it.

They were rich. The whole thing had been quite a gamble, but it had paid off.

Now all they had to do was get the gold out of that rock wall. . . .

As he rode across the canyon, angling toward the Hampton claim, Milo couldn't believe his good luck. Finally, after all this time, he had done something right, and it was going to pay off.

In a strange way, he thought, it was lucky he had tried to bushwhack John Fury.

It was just too bad his brother Johnny couldn't be here to share in the good fortune with him.

That thought sobered Milo for a few minutes and wiped the grin off his face, but slowly it crept back onto his features. He was indeed a lucky man. Not only was he going to have more money than he'd ever dreamed of, but he knew now that the time had finally come to tell Nora what was on his mind and in his heart. His days as a jinx were over, so he could ask her to marry him without having to worry about what might happen to her.

Of course, he might be wrong about the way she felt, he realized. She might say no when he asked her. He didn't know what he'd do if that happened!

Milo was brooding about that and almost didn't notice when a man rode past a couple of hundred yards in front of him, moving fast.

The sound of thudding hoofbeats finally penetrated Milo's distracted brain, however, and he reined his horse to a stop in time to see another rider disappearing into a stand of trees. Milo frowned. He was pretty sure the other man had been Will Corey, and he wondered where Corey was going in such a hurry.

Maybe there was more trouble, another raid by the Hell-hounds or some other group of bad men. Milo put his horse into a trot again and rode toward the spot where Corey had vanished. This little detour wouldn't take him long, and he knew Fury would want him to find out what was going on, especially if something was wrong.

Milo rode through the trees and spotted Corey going up a distant rise, still moving fast. Indecision made Milo's frown deepen. Go after Corey, or head back to the Hampton place to get that blasting powder? Going back was the smart thing to do, Milo thought.

Yet every instinct told him to keep trailing Corey. In the past, Milo's instincts had been so bad, so often wrong, that he had sometimes tried to figure out the best thing to do, then done just the opposite. But that usually hadn't worked, either, because you couldn't trick fate.

"Well, hell," he said out loud, wishing he'd never even noticed Corey.

Then he spurred ahead, following the mayor.

Almost before Milo knew it, he had reached the northern end of the canyon. Corey was still up ahead. Milo had given up on catching him and had deliberately dropped back a little instead, letting Corey stretch the lead out. Why he was doing that, Milo couldn't have said, but he knew that Fury didn't much like Will Corey, and if Fury was suspicious of somebody, that was enough for Milo.

Corey led him into the rough country beyond the canyon, and Milo kept hanging back so that he couldn't be easily spotted. A couple of times, he thought he had lost Corey's trail, but then he caught sight of the man again and kept going. Finally, Corey entered a stand of pine trees . . . and didn't come out again.

There was a ridge off to the right of the trees. Milo headed for it, circling around to come up on the far side from the spot where Corey had disappeared. He was taking a chance on the mayor giving him the slip, he knew, but he couldn't see any way of getting close enough to find out what was going on without using the ridge for cover. He left his horse at the base of the slope and started climbing.

He reached the top in time to see two more men on horseback entering the trees. Milo didn't recognize either of them, but he could follow their progress easily enough through the screen of pine needles and trunks. From this angle, he could see down into a small clearing as the two strangers entered one side of it and Will Corey rode out from the other.

"What do you want?" Corey asked, the question coming plainly to Milo's ears as the young man crouched at the top of the ridge. "I got your message, but I don't much like meeting in the daylight like this."

"Take it easy, Corey," one of the other men said. "We're quite a ways from Last Chance Canyon, so I don't think anybody back there will know you've been meetin' us."

"Well, get on with it, Sullivan," Corey snapped.

The man leaned forward in his saddle. "Duncan and me, we was wonderin' when you're goin' to have all the troublemakers cleaned out o' the area."

"Soon. The vigilantes have gotten rid of the Jeffords boys and that other bunch that drifted in. They all cooperated by pulling robberies, just like we thought they might. I didn't even have to plant any phony evidence to convince the others to string them up."

Milo gaped in astonishment at what he was hearing from Corey. Taking his cue from Fury, he didn't much like the man, either, but he never would have dreamed that Corey was working with the Hellhounds. Milo knew who the two strangers were now: Mike Sullivan and Duncan Laidlaw, the leaders of the gang. Had to be. He had heard all about them from Fury, Joe, Ben Hampton, and some of the other miners who'd had run-ins with the Hellhounds.

Laidlaw grinned and said, "This is a pretty good deal you cooked up, Corey, usin' vigilance committees to clean out all the competition so that the Hellhounds can take over. Just don't get too ambitious and start thinkin' about double-crossin' us. You won't live long if you try to pull somethin' like that, mate."

"Don't worry," Corey said. "We all have the same objective in mind, after all. And it's almost within our grasp, gentlemen, almost within our grasp."

Milo leaned forward a little more, trying to catch every word. His elbow brushed a rock and dislodged it. He jerked back in surprise, then lunged forward and grabbed for the falling rock.

And missed.

This was the second landslide Milo Phipps had started, and it was on a much smaller scale than the first one. But it was equally as dangerous, because Corey, Sullivan, and Laidlaw all heard the sudden clattering cascade of stones down the ridge, and they jerked their guns out as they turned to look for the source of the noise.

Milo scrambled back, his brain whirling. He had to get out of here, had to get back to the canyon and warn the others that Corey was betraying them to the Hellhounds. Besides, if they caught him, they'd kill him, sure as hell.

He lurched to his feet and turned to run back down the slope.

"There!" Corey cried.

He shouldn't have gotten up where they could see him, Milo realized. His instincts had double-crossed him again, just like countless times in the past. He had to duck down out of sight. . . .

Three guns blasted behind him, and something slammed into Milo's back, high up toward his left shoulder. The force of the blow knocked him forward, and he fell hard, tumbling down the far side of the ridge. The world spun crazily, sky and ground swapping places a dozen times as he rolled down the slope. His head banged against rocks, and each blow sent him spiraling deeper into a red and black maelstrom. Waves of pain washed out from his wounded shoulder and carried him along.

They carried him right into a dark, endless sea where he sank without a trace, and his last thought as the blackness claimed him was a simple, bitter one:

Once a Jonah, always a Jonah.

CHAPTER
15

....

Milo had no idea how long he had been unconscious. All he knew was that he was still alive. He was hurting *way* too much to be dead.

The whole left side of his body was a mass of pain. He was lying on his back, and he rolled onto his right side to put less pressure on the wound. For some reason, now that he was awake again, he was thinking clearly, maybe more clearly than he ever had before. Maybe it was the pain itself that was forcing him to concentrate, sweeping away all the distractions of guilt and memory.

Corey and the two Hellhounds had tried to kill him. They would certainly accomplish that goal if they found him, wounded and helpless like this.

Milo rolled again, onto his belly this time. He got his right hand underneath him, and then he tried to pull his knees up. Slowly, he forced them into position, then heaved himself up on them, balancing himself with the good hand.

Sunlight beat down on him, and as he rested for a moment after that effort, he could hear birds singing and small animals moving around in the brush. That told him he had been out cold for a while. The birds and animals had had time to return after being frightened off by the burst of gunfire.

Where were Sullivan, Laidlaw, and Corey? Surely they had come looking for him. With everything they had at stake, they wouldn't just assume that he was dead. They would want to be absolutely positive.

He had to get moving, Milo thought, had to get out of there. But at the same time, he had to be careful. If the three killers hadn't found him so far, he didn't want to carelessly reveal himself to them.

He lifted his head and looked around, blinking against the light that struck his eyes almost like a blow. He was surrounded by brush, and although it obscured his vision somewhat, he could tell that he was at the bottom of a small gully. How he had gotten there he didn't know. Either he had rolled into it following his breakneck spill down the ridge, or his instinct for survival had been working even though he was out of his head with pain and he had pulled himself into the makeshift hiding place. Milo didn't know and didn't care which possibility was true.

Where was his horse?

If he could get mounted again, maybe he could get back to the canyon and find somebody to help him. He would be able to get away from Corey, Sullivan, and Laidlaw a lot easier on horseback than on foot, he knew that.

"Where the hell did he go?"

"I don't know. But he's around here somewhere. Keep looking."

The voices were faint and distant, but Milo heard them well enough to recognize the second one as belonging to Will Corey. They were searching for him, all right, and he had to get moving now if he wanted to get away.

Slowly, Milo started crawling in the opposite direction from the voices. He stayed in the sun-dappled gully and moved cautiously enough so that he didn't make much noise creeping along the carpet of dead leaves on the bottom of the gully. He listened intently for signs of the pursuit getting closer to him, and that concentration helped him block out the pain from his wounded shoulder.

Just as he didn't know how long he had been unconscious, he wasn't sure how much time was passing as he crawled along the gully. Time didn't seem to have much meaning at the moment. He kept moving somehow, even when it seemed that the last of his strength was going to desert him.

He had to live, had to get back to the canyon and warn the others that Corey was going to betray them. . . .

Suddenly, he heard a snuffling sound and paused to try to figure out what it was. The noise came again, and this time he recognized it as the blowing of a nervous horse. His horse, maybe? Milo crawled over to the edge of the gully and used the bank to pull himself more upright.

Yes, there it was! It was his horse, all right, trailing some broken reins. The shooting had spooked it, and it had pulled free from the tree where he had tied it earlier before climbing up the ridge to spy on Corey and the others. Milo clambered up out of the gully, his left arm dangling uselessly and still dripping blood, and he called softly, "Here, boy! It's just me, boy!"

His voice sounded hoarse and wrong to him, and it must have to the horse, too, because the animal shied away. It probably smelled the blood on him, as well, and that wouldn't make things any easier. Milo knew he was in no shape to have to chase after the horse, so he tried again, talking to it in as calm a tone as he could manage.

Something in his voice must have gotten through to the animal, because it finally stood still as Milo stumbled toward it. He caught the broken reins and then leaned against the horse, hanging on to the saddle horn to keep him upright. He had to rest that way for several minutes before he felt up to even attempting to get into the saddle. Balancing himself carefully, he lifted his left foot and got it into the stirrup, then took a deep breath and pulled himself up.

He sprawled awkwardly into the saddle, almost slipped off, and caught himself at the last second before falling. Settling himself, he managed to get both feet in the stirrups and kept his grip on the saddle horn. His heels bumped feebly against the flanks of the horse, just enough to nudge it into motion. It started off in a slow walk toward the south.

Well, at least that was the right direction, Milo thought. Now if Corey and the Hellhounds didn't spot him . . . if he could get back to Last Chance Canyon without passing out and falling off the horse . . . if he could find somebody who would believe him when he told them about Corey, somebody who would help him . . .

Nora. Nora would help him. She and her father and her brothers were his only hope. He knew he couldn't make it all the way back to Joe's claim.

But maybe when he didn't return with the blasting powder, they would come looking for him. He had a chance, Milo thought. He couldn't give up yet. So he'd had a little bad luck and gotten himself shot. Luck could change, couldn't it?

Grimly, Milo kept riding.

"Where the hell has Milo gotten off to?" Fury asked. "He should have been back from Hampton's a long time ago."

Joe leaned on his pick handle and wiped sweat off his face. "Yeah, I was thinking the same thing," he said as he paused in the work of chipping away at the canyon wall. "Reckon he ran into trouble?"

"I can take one of the horses and go looking for him," J. D. offered.

Fury shook his head. "You don't need to be riding around the canyon by yourself."

"I'd be fine," she protested. "You've seen how I can handle a gun. There's no need for you to protect me."

"Maybe not, but I'd feel better if you stayed here with Joe." Fury dropped his pick and reached for his shirt. "I'll go see if I can find him."

"That's a good idea," Joe said. "J. D. and I will stay here and keep working."

J. D. stepped forward and lifted the pick Fury had dropped. "It's time I take my turn at this," she said determinedly. "I can swing a pick—especially to help uncover a vein the size of this one."

Fury wasn't going to argue with her about that. He was worried about Milo Phipps. A hard-luck case like Milo could usually find trouble even in places where most people wouldn't. Not only that, but with the Hellhounds still operating in the area, nobody riding alone was completely safe, no matter who they were.

He got the heavy Sharps carbine from the tent and carried it over to the corral, then saddled the dun and slipped the rifle into the saddleboot. "Be back in a little while," he called to Joe and J. D., then sent the horse loping easily toward Ben Hampton's claim. The sweat on his body had quickly soaked into his shirt, and the wind of his passage was pleasantly cooling.

The ground was too rocky here to hold many tracks, and although Fury was able to follow Milo's trail for a short distance, he soon lost it. He couldn't imagine where Milo might have gone except Hampton's. The youngster would have been anxious not only to fetch the blasting powder but to see Nora as well.

By the time he reached Hampton's place, Fury hadn't seen any sign of Milo. Nora and Orville were in back of the cabin working in the small garden. Hampton, Dave, and Thurl emerged from the shaft as Fury rode up. Hampton lifted a hand in greeting and called, "Howdy, John. What brings you over here?"

"Looking for Milo Phipps, Ben," Fury replied. "Have you seen him today?"

Hampton frowned and shook his head. "Milo? Can't say as I have. What about you boys?"

Dave and Thurl shook their heads, too.

Nora and Orville had come around the cabin to join them, and they arrived in time for Nora to hear Fury's question. "What's this about Milo?" she asked. "Is something wrong, Mr. Fury?"

"Don't know yet, Miss Nora. He started over here a couple of hours ago to see if he could buy some of your blasting powder, and he never came back."

"Milo hasn't been here at all today," Nora said, an anxious frown appearing on her pretty face. "I'd know if he had been."

"Where the devil could the boy be?" Hampton wondered. "You don't reckon he's up and run off on you, do you, John?"

Fury hesitated before answering. Under the circumstances, he was certain Milo wouldn't have left for good. Not with a share in what looked to be a rich lode waiting for him. But did Fury want to mention that to the Hamptons?

On the other hand, a man couldn't distrust everybody all the time, and Ben Hampton and his family had never shown signs of being anything except loyal friends. Fury swung down from his saddle and said, "Milo wouldn't run off. Not now. Not after what we found today." He went on to explain about the vein of gold they had uncovered.

Hampton let out a low whistle. "Sounds like a bonanza, all right. But if that's the case, what's happened to Milo?"

Nora let out a scream in answer.

The men whirled around to see what was wrong. Nora was pointing a shaky finger toward the north end of the canyon. She had brought her other hand, clenched into a fist, to her mouth. She was staring at a figure on horseback, riding toward them hunched over the saddle, the horse following a rather erratic path.

"That's Milo!" Fury exclaimed, running forward to meet the youngster. As he grabbed the horse's dangling reins, he saw the huge bloodstain on the left side of Milo's shirt.

Hampton and his sons gathered around as Fury led the horse with its grisly burden up to the cabin. Nora cried, "Get him down off of there! Be careful!"

"Take it easy, gal," Hampton told his daughter calmly. "We know what to do. Ain't like this is the first gun-shot man we ever seen."

"It's the first time *Milo's* been shot," Nora replied raggedly. "Bring him inside."

With the help of Dave and Thurl, Fury eased Milo down from the saddle and carried him into the cabin. Ordering them sharply not to worry about the blankets on the bunk, Nora told them to put him down on her bed. They did so, and as Dave and Thurl stepped back, Fury drew his Bowie knife and began cutting away Milo's shirt, which was red and sodden with blood.

"Let me help—" Nora began.

"Ben, you'd better keep Nora back," Fury broke in. "I've patched up bullet wounds before, so I know what I'm doing. Going to need hot water and plenty of cloths."

"Sort of like birthin' a baby," Hampton said. "Boys, take your sister outside and get a fire goin'. Take a pot for the water with you. Nora, start tearin' up some blankets."

She nodded, fighting back tears, and went outside with her brothers.

"Bullet punched clean through," Fury muttered to himself when he had laid the wound bare. "That's lucky. Might've chipped the collarbone a little, but doesn't seem to have shattered it. That's good, too. But the boy's lost a hell of a lot of blood."

"What're you goin' to do, John?" Hampton asked.

"Clean up those bullet holes, bandage them, and hope for the best. That's about all we can do."

Fury tossed his hat aside, and when Thurl brought him the first of the rags soaked in hot water a few minutes later, he started swabbing away the blood, both the dried stuff and the drops that were still oozing from the wound. Without being asked, Hampton dug a bottle of whiskey out of a trunk and offered it to Fury, who pulled the cork and doused the wounds, front and back, with the fiery stuff. Milo was out cold, but he still moaned as the whiskey burned into the raw flesh.

Nora and her brothers slipped back into the room, and although Fury knew they were there, he didn't run them out again. He was well aware of how Nora and Milo felt about each other, and he didn't want to make things worse for her. However, he didn't say anything until the wounds were tightly bandaged and Milo was lying on his right side in the bunk, breathing deeply and regularly despite his unconsciousness.

Fury felt his muscles and bones creaking as he stood up from where he had been crouched at the bedside. He was getting too old for this, he thought. Then he smiled at Nora and the others and said, "His heart's thumping along like a steam engine, and he's breathing good. I think he's going to be all right."

"Thank the Lord!" Nora breathed. "And you, too, Mr. Fury. I'm so glad you were here."

"Milo's going to need a lot of care," Fury warned her. "After losing that much blood, he's going to be mighty weak for a long time. Reckon I can count on you to help take care of him?"

"You know you can," Nora said quietly but fervently.

Fury grinned. "Thought so."

Hampton said, "Question now is, who shot the boy?"

"I wish I knew," Fury said with a shake of his head. "Hellhounds, probably."

"Not . . . just . . . Hellhounds," came a hoarse whisper from the bunk.

Fury spun around. He'd been unaware until now that Milo had regained consciousness. As he dropped to his knees beside the bed again, he said, "Take it easy, boy. You'd better not try to talk."

"Got . . . got to," insisted Milo, blinking up at Fury through eyes made bleary by shock and loss of blood. "Got to . . . tell you . . . about Corey . . ."

"Will Corey?" Fury exclaimed in surprise. He leaned closer. "What about Corey?"

"Working with . . . Hellhounds . . . b-betraying us all . . . ." Milo started breathing harder.

Fury put a hand on his uninjured shoulder. "Settle down, Milo," he said firmly. "Don't work yourself up into a state. That'll just make things worse."

Milo closed his eyes for a moment and drew a deep breath, wincing against the pain that racked him. Then he looked up at Fury again and said in a clearer voice, "I saw Corey . . . talking to Sullivan and Laidlaw. . . . Heard him say they've been working together . . . all along."

"That son of a bitch!" Ben Hampton exclaimed. "And we all thought he was helpin' us. Mayor of Last Chance Canyon, my foot!"

"Got to . . . stop him, Mr. Fury." Milo raised his good hand and closed his fingers over Fury's forearm in an urgent grip. "Got to . . . do something about him."

"I will, Milo," Fury said grimly. "I can promise you that."

"Good," the wounded man murmured. His eyes closed again, and his head slipped back a little. Nora let out a little gasp, thinking for an instant that Milo had died before realizing that he had just gone to sleep.

"Let him rest," Fury said as he stood up. "Then, as soon as you can, get some food and water down him. Nothing but broth at first, until he gets some of his strength back."

"I understand," Nora said. "Don't worry, Mr. Fury, I'll take good care of him."

Fury smiled at her. "I'm sure you will." He turned to Hampton and the three younger men. "You fellas get ready to ride. I'm going back to the claim to get Joe, and then we'll come back by here. It's time we had a showdown with Corey."

"Damn right," Hampton said. "We'll be ready, John."

Fury went outside, mounted up, and sent the dun galloping back toward Joe's claim. He wondered what J. D. was going to say when she heard that Will Corey was nothing but a lying, double-crossing skunk. She probably wouldn't believe it at first.

But it didn't really matter. Like Fury had told Hampton, it was time to put an end to the threat of Will Corey and the Hellhounds.

Corey was burning with anger as he rode back through the canyon. Although he, Laidlaw, and Sullivan had searched for over an hour, they had been unable to find Milo Phipps. Corey was pretty sure that Phipps was dead—he had seen the blood where one of the slugs hit Phipps in the back—but it would have been nice to find the body and put a few more bullets into it, just to make certain.

Laidlaw and Sullivan hadn't been particularly worried. "The bastard's just crawled off somewhere to die," the Irishman had said offhandedly as he and Laidlaw got ready to ride back to the roadhouse that served as their headquarters. "Don't worry about it, Corey. Your secret's still safe."

Corey wished he could be sure of that. After all, Sullivan and Laidlaw could afford to be nonchalant about this problem. They hadn't spent months building up a respectable image the way Corey had. The miners in Last Chance Canyon trusted him. He knew which claims were paying off and which ones weren't, where the resistance might be and which miners could be counted on to cave in under pressure. When the time came for the Hellhounds to make their final sweep through the canyon, the information gathered by Corey would serve them well.

Then he'd be a rich man, richer by far than he ever would have become if he'd stayed back in Vermont, trying to pound some knowledge into the thickheaded sons of thicker-headed bankers and businessmen.

For years, Corey had seen them come and go, and he knew he was smarter than any of them, smarter than any of their fathers. It was unfair that they had so much more money when they were so deficient in every other area. So he had given up and come out here to California, following the tales of wealth that came from the area, and he had found that life out here was patently unfair, too. "Dumb luck" became a phrase with more meaning than ever when he saw how one man's claim could pay off and another man's next to it could be totally worthless.

Intelligence might not mean nearly as much when it came to finding gold, but he had been smart enough to set up the arrangement with Sullivan and Laidlaw. And it was going to make him rich where none of his previous endeavors had.

Still uneasy, however, Corey rode toward Joe Brackett's claim. Surely that was where Phipps would have gone, if he

had somehow survived being shot. Corey had to know whether or not his masquerade as an honest miner and community
leader had been exposed. There was only one way to do that.
He had to find out if Phipps was still alive.

As he approached the claim, Corey spotted Brackett and
J. D. McKavett working at the canyon wall with picks and
shovels. There didn't seem to be anyone else around. And
Brackett and J. D. didn't appear to be upset when they turned
around, warned by the sound of his horse's hoofbeats, and
saw him coming. Both of them lifted a hand in greeting.

Corey rode across the creek, reined in, and grinned at them.
"Good afternoon," he called. "How are you today?"

"Fine," J. D. replied. She glanced over at Brackett. "More
than fine."

Corey caught some extra meaning in her words, and he
saw the small frown of disapproval on Brackett's face, spotted the tiny shake of the black man's head. Brackett was trying to warn J. D. not to say too much. Too much about what?

Corey looked past them at the cliff face, and there was no
need for more questions. He could see the answer gleaming
there, plain as day.

"My word!" Corey exclaimed involuntarily. "That's quite
a rich vein you've uncovered there."

"A bonanza," J. D. said, excitement in her voice. She looked
at Brackett and went on. "Don't worry, Joe. I'm sure we can
trust Mr. Corey not to spread the news of our discovery too
soon."

"That's right, Brackett," Corey assured him. "I can keep
quiet when I need to."

And he would certainly keep quiet about this, Corey
thought. He wasn't about to share this with Sullivan and
Laidlaw. They could have the leftover pickings in the rest
of the canyon.

As soon as he had seen the way the light hit that gold,
Will Corey had known it was going to be his, all his.

He swung down from the saddle, his brain working furiously as he tried to keep up with the greed exploding inside

him. He summoned up a smile and said, "Could I talk to you for a moment, J. D.? In private?"

"Well . . ." She hesitated. "I suppose so. You don't mind, do you, Joe?"

"We've been working pretty hard," Brackett told her. "A couple minutes rest won't hurt either of us."

"Thank you." J. D. smiled at Corey, linked arms with him, and as they strolled toward the creek, she said, "I'm all yours."

"That's exactly what I want to talk to you about, J. D.," Corey said, trying to sound as sincere as he could. "I've grown rather fond of you, as you may know." He kept his voice pitched low enough so that Brackett couldn't overhear what he was saying. "I think you're a remarkable woman, and I'd like to share the rest of my life with you."

J. D. stopped, blinked at him in surprise, and began tentatively, "Will, are you asking me—"

"I'm asking you to marry me, J. D."

It was all so simple, Corey thought. He would marry J. D. McKavett, and then her share of the claim would be equally his. If Milo Phipps had a share, it would be a small one, and anyway, Phipps was dead, Corey told himself. As for Fury and Brackett . . .

Well, once he and J. D. were safely married, Fury and Brackett could meet with accidents. And when they were dead, this claim and all its riches would belong solely to J. D.

And to him, Will Corey, as well. Will Corey, who would soon enough become a grieving—but rich—widower. . . .

All J. D. had to do was say—

"No, Will, I'm sorry. I can't marry you."

Corey felt like somebody had just punched him in the belly. He all but gasped for breath as he said, "What?"

"I can't marry you, Will," J. D. repeated. "I like you a great deal and I certainly admire you, but I . . . I just don't love you."

"Love?" Corey's voice rose wildly without him even being aware of it. "What the hell does love have to do with it? I'm talking about gold!"

J. D. drew away from him, looking at him with a startled expression on her face. "Will, this isn't like you—"

"Isn't like me? What do you know about me?" Out of the corner of his eye, Corey saw Brackett coming toward them, a look of alarm on his face now that Corey was shouting. Rage exploded in Corey's head, just as greed had filled his mind earlier. He said, "You're going to marry me, and I'm going to be a rich man!"

"Back off, Corey!" Brackett said. "Leave the lady alone—"

Corey spun to face the young black man, and only the fact that Brackett wasn't expecting such a move enabled Corey to pull his gun and center it on Brackett's chest. Corey was no gunslinger, but he *was* a desperate man. "Stay back!" he cried. "This is none of your business, nigger!"

"Will! You can't talk like that to Joe—"

"Shut up! You're going to marry me, and that's all there is to it."

"You're crazy, mister," Brackett said.

"Crazy, am I?" And as Corey snarled the words, the barrel of his pistol started to lift and his finger began to tighten on the trigger.

A gun boomed, somewhere across the creek.

A heavy slug whipped past Corey's head, and his finger jerked reflexively on the trigger in response. The pistol blasted, sending a bullet toward Joe Brackett, who dived to the side and clawed for his own gun. He couldn't fire, though, because Corey had already grabbed J. D., who had been frozen in shock, and yanked her in front of him.

"Come on, damn it!"

Corey hauled her with him as he ran toward his horse. A glance up the canyon told him that John Fury was the one who had fired the first shot. Fury had sheathed the Sharps and was now riding hell-for-leather toward the claim on that rangy dun of his. Corey knew somehow that Fury was aware of what he had done, and he knew, too, that his only hope for escape was J. D.

He dragged her toward his horse and shoved her up into the saddle. Brackett snapped a shot toward him that burned across the rump of Corey's mount. He hung on desperately to the animal and half-turned to fire at Brackett again. The shot missed, but it came close enough to send Brackett diving for cover again. Corey swung up on the horse, clamped an arm around J. D. in a brutal grip, and holstered his gun in order to grab the reins. Banging his heels against the animal's flanks, he sent it racing off to the northwest, following the canyon wall away from the claim, away from Brackett and Fury.

They couldn't shoot at him, not without risking J. D.'s life as well. And they wouldn't do that. With his superior intelligence, Corey was certain of that. He was still going to win, he told himself. He was smart enough to figure a way out of this disaster.

The roadhouse—if he could just get to the roadhouse! Sullivan and Laidlaw would help him. They had been spoiling for a chance to go on a rampage. Well, the time had come, Corey decided.

Before this day was over, there would be war in Last Chance Canyon.

CHAPTER
16
....

When Fury reached the camp, he leaped down from his horse and ran over to Joe, who was just picking himself up and brushing himself off. "What the devil's going on?" the young man asked. "Corey seemed to just go crazy when he saw that vein of gold!"

"He's been working with the Hellhounds all along," Fury explained, feeling a surge of relief as he saw that Joe was all right. "Milo saw him talking to Sullivan and Laidlaw, and they tried to kill the kid. Shot him in the back."

"Damn! Where's Milo now?"

"At the Hampton place," Fury said. "He managed to get back there, and I patched him as best I could. I think he'll be all right. We've got something else to worry about now, though."

"J. D.," Joe said bleakly.

Fury nodded. "Corey's probably heading toward that roadhouse. He figures the Hellhounds will take him in now that we know he's been lying all along. And he took J. D. with him to use as a hostage until he thinks he's safe." Fury wheeled and started back toward his horse. Over his shoulder, he told Joe, "Go get Ben Hampton and his boys and anybody else you can find. I'll be at the roadhouse."

"John," Joe called after him, "don't do anything foolish. You can't go up against that whole gang by yourself."

"Don't worry about me," Fury said. "Just get Hampton and the others and come as quick as you can."

He swung up into the saddle and sent the dun off in a gallop, following the curve of the canyon as Corey had done a few minutes earlier. Fury didn't know how fast Corey's horse was, but the animal was carrying double, and there was still a chance Fury could catch up before Corey and J. D. reached the roadhouse.

He urged all the speed out of the dun that he could. If he had angled toward the canyon wall when Corey had fled, the man might never have gotten away, but Fury had seen the exchange of shots at the camp and hadn't been able to tell if Joe was hit or not. It had been a hard decision, but Fury had come on to the claim to make sure Joe was all right before pursuing Corey.

And now, because of that decision, J. D.'s life hung in the balance.

Fury figured he would at least catch sight of them before they reached the roadhouse, but by the time Cougar Bluff and the log building beneath that looming shelf of rock came into view, he hadn't seen Corey or J. D. Corey knew this canyon better than he did, and the renegade mayor must have taken some shortcuts that brought him to the roadhouse sooner. Fury was sure they were there; he recognized Corey's mount, tied up among the horses at the hitch rack in front of the roadhouse.

While he was still out of rifle range, Fury reined in and studied the roadhouse. Nobody was moving around outside. Corey was probably inside telling Sullivan, Laidlaw, and the other renegades how he had lost his head. They likely didn't know that Milo was still alive and could bring other evidence against them. None of that really mattered now, however. The important thing was figuring a way to get J. D. out of there safely.

The door of the roadhouse opened and several men hurried out, heading toward the horses. Maybe the Hellhounds weren't going to wait for more trouble to come to them, Fury thought. Maybe they were going to launch an attack against the miners so that they could get in the first blow. Fury couldn't let that happen. He slid the Sharps out of its sheath, opened the breech, and slipped one of the long cartridges from his belt into the chamber. Snapping it shut, he lifted the heavy carbine to his shoulder.

A second later, the Sharps boomed, and one of the men who was reaching for his horse's reins felt the slug pluck his hat right off his head. Howling curses, the man ducked back, stumbled, and fell. His companions ran back to the safety of the building, and the man whose hat Fury had shot off scrambled to his feet and followed them frantically. All of them disappeared inside, and the door slammed behind them.

Fury grinned faintly as he reloaded the Sharps. He was going to do his best to keep them pinned down until reinforcements got here.

Of course, it was going to be hard to pry them out of there. The roadhouse was sturdily built, and if the Hellhounds had enough ammunition, food, and water in there, as was likely, they could hold off any number of attackers for quite a while.

And they still had J. D. to use as a trump card.

The grin faded from Fury's face. He had to think of something to change the odds, otherwise things were liable to get a lot worse. . . .

Fury had worked his way into a clump of good-sized rocks about a hundred yards from the roadhouse by the time Joe and the others got there. A few shots had come his way from the building, but not many. The Hellhounds seemed content to lie low for the moment. When Fury heard the approaching hoofbeats, he turned and raised himself enough to wave to the riders to take cover.

Sure enough, more gunfire erupted from the roadhouse, sending slugs whistling over the heads of the men on horseback. They dropped quickly from their saddles and ran forward, leaving the horses with a couple of men who would take the mounts back out of range. Fury saw Joe, Ben Hampton, the Hampton boys, and about two dozen other miners, some of whom he had gotten to know fairly well in the past couple of months, some of them virtual strangers. But they had all banded together to help J. D. and to try to rid Last Chance Canyon of the menace of the Hellhounds.

"Any sign of J. D.?" Joe asked as he dropped into a crouch beside Fury.

"I haven't seen her," Fury replied. "But Corey's horse is there, and I'm sure she's inside with him. That's why we can't just open up on the place and fill it full of lead. Too good a chance a stray shot would hit her." Fury raised his voice so that the other men could hear him. "Hold your fire for now, and keep your heads down!"

"What can we do, John?" Ben Hampton asked. "We can't let Corey get away with betrayin' us, and Joe says he's got Miz McKavett a prisoner in there, too!"

"That's right," Fury said with a grim nod. "I reckon what we've got on our hands is a siege."

"There's a back door to that place," Joe suggested. "I could try to slip in there and get J. D. out."

Fury shook his head. "That'd be a good way to get you and her both killed right off. I'm not ready to risk that. I've been thinking, and I may have an idea. . . ."

Quickly, Fury outlined his plan. When he was finished, Joe and Hampton both frowned dubiously. "I don't know," Joe said. "Seems mighty risky."

"But it may be the only chance we have," Fury pointed out, and neither of the other men could argue with that.

The plan would take some time to put into effect, though, and until then, all they could do was wait.

Wait . . . and pray.

Thirty minutes had passed, and the sun was beginning to slide down toward the western horizon. It would be dark in another hour, and that was a growing concern of Fury's. If the standoff continued until after night fell, the Hellhounds might be able to slip out of the roadhouse with their prisoner. This fracas was going to have to come to a conclusion soon.

A few slugs had whined off the rocks behind which the miners were hidden, but nobody had been hit. They had been lucky so far, and Fury knew it.

But luck was a fragile thing, as Milo Phipps had proven more than once, and it could always change for the worse.

Suddenly, the sound of hoofbeats came to Fury's ears, and he jerked his head around to see who was coming. The rider was in a hurry; that much was obvious. He spotted the man coming toward the rocks and quirting his mount into a dead run.

"Gold! Whoooeee! Big gold strike in Frenchman's Gulch! Gold!"

Fury's face was drawn into a tight mask as the man slid off his horse and ran forward, heedless of the danger he might be placing himself in. When gold fever got hold of a man, he sometimes forgot about everything else. Fury recognized the newcomer as one of the miners from down the canyon.

In a loud, exuberant voice, the man kept crying out, "Gold in Frenchman's Gulch! The biggest bonanza yet! We got to get over there, boys!"

The men crouched behind the rocks began to stir restlessly and cast furtive glances toward Fury.

"No!" Fury shouted. "Don't pay any attention to him, goddammit! We've finally got the Hellhounds where we want them. We've got 'em trapped! You can't go running off just because there's a new strike somewhere!"

Ben Hampton looked uncomfortable. "We've all been tryin' to find a good vein ever since we been out here, John. You heard what that fella said. It's a bonanza! We can't afford to pass it up." He came up into a crouch, waved his rifle at the other men, and called, "Me an' my boys are pullin' out and headin' for Frenchman's Gulch! If you got any sense, you better come with me!" Then he ran for the horses without looking back, taking Dave and Orville with him.

That was all it took to break the resolve of the other men. Wiping out a band of criminals and rescuing a woman was all well and good, but it couldn't compete with the lure of gold. With howls of excitement and anticipation, they abandoned their hiding places and retreated toward the spot where their horses were waiting. Gold fever had all of them in its irresistable grip.

All of them except Fury and Joe Brackett. "Come back here, blast it!" Fury bellowed. "You can't just leave that woman a prisoner in there—"

"Forget it, John," Joe advised. "It's just you and me now."

Fury took a deep breath and watched wordlessly as the group of miners quickly mounted up and galloped off in search of riches, leaving nothing behind but the sound of fading hoofbeats and a cloud of dust in the air.

"Fury!"

The shout from the roadhouse made Fury's head jerk around again. He recognized the voice as Will Corey's. Keeping a tight rein on his temper, he called back, "What do you want, Corey? You ready to surrender?"

"Surrender, hell!" Corey replied, good humor plain to hear in his tone. "You just lost your army, Fury! We heard and saw most of that, and we know there's nobody left out there except you and the nigger. You're the ones who'd better give up!"

"Forget it!" Fury slid the barrel of the Sharps over the rock behind which he crouched and touched off a shot that thudded into the porch of the roadhouse. "We've still got you pinned down in there!"

For a moment there was silence from the roadhouse, then abruptly the door of the place swung open. "Hold your fire!" Corey yelled.

Behind the rocks, Joe said in a low voice, "He's not surrendering."

"Never expected him to," Fury replied without taking his eyes off the dark rectangle of the open doorway.

Figures appeared in it, and he recognized the light-colored shirt J. D. had been wearing and the fair hair tumbling around her shoulders. She was forced out into the open, one arm held painfully behind her. Corey had that tight grip on her, and with his other hand he held a pistol to her head. As the two of them came out of the roadhouse, Sullivan and Laidlaw followed them. The two leaders of the Hellhounds both held pistols ready for instant use.

"Don't try anything, Fury!" Sullivan warned. "Even if you got lucky enough to drop all three of us without hittin' the lady, our boys inside got their rifles trained on her. She dies unless you an' your darkie friend do what we tell you."

Fury put a hand on Joe's arm and felt the tension there. "Like he says, take it easy," Fury said. "Let's see what they want." Lifting his voice again, he called out, "Let's hear it!"

"Come out where we can see you!" Laidlaw ordered.

"So you can shoot us down? Not hardly!"

Corey said, "You've got our word you won't be harmed if you cooperate. Besides"—he pushed the barrel of his pistol against J. D.'s temple and made her cry out in pain—"you don't have a lot of choice, do you? Come out of those rocks, or I'll kill her!"

"John . . . ?" Joe breathed.

Fury glanced up at the bluff above the roadhouse, his rugged features bleak. Then he heaved a deep sigh and said, "He's right. We don't have any choice."

Gripping the big revolver tightly in his right hand, Fury rose and stepped out from behind the cover of the rocks. Joe did likewise, and side by side, they began walking slowly toward Corey, Sullivan, Laidlaw, and J. D.

"You've got us where you want us," Fury told the trio of outlaws. "Let J. D. out of here."

Corey jerked his head from side to side and pushed J. D. forward. She stumbled a little but kept on her feet. Followed by Sullivan and Laidlaw, Corey and J. D. advanced to meet Fury and Joe. Behind them, several more of the Hellhounds emerged from the roadhouse. The owner of the place also scurried out and started up the canyon on foot, obviously relieved he had gotten a chance to get out of the place before any more shooting started.

"Nobody's going anywhere yet," Corey said. "Not until we have everything we want."

"And what's that?" Joe asked.

"That claim of yours, nigger." Corey sneered. "I don't know how big that strike over in Frenchman's Gulch is, but I'd wager it's not as big as the one you made today. You're going to sign that claim over to me all nice and legal-like, Brackett, otherwise J. D. dies. That shelf of gold is going to be *mine*!"

"Hey, what about us?" Sullivan asked suddenly. "We're partners, ain't we?"

"Of course, of course," Corey snapped, his voice impatient. "I'd never try to cut the two of you out of anything." His eyes bored into Joe. "What about it, Brackett? Do you cooperate and maybe live . . . or do we just kill all of you and take what we want? Either way, we wind up with the gold!"

Fury and Joe exchanged a quick glance. Both of them knew that Corey couldn't be trusted. Joe could sign over the claim and still wind up dead, along with Fury and J. D. After everything that had happened, the Hellhounds couldn't afford to let them live.

"I reckon it's time," Fury said quietly.

His left hand went to his hat and lifted it over his head.

"Watch out!" Sullivan yelled. "It's some kind of trick! Kill them!"

For a split second, Fury thought everything had gone wrong. If that was the case, he and Joe would sell their lives as dearly as possible, and J. D. would not die without being avenged.

But then the world shook under their feet, and the sound of a huge explosion slammed into their ears with deafening force.

High above the roadhouse, Cougar Bluff trembled for a few seconds, then massive slabs of rock began to break off and fall. The avalanche grew in force as the entire bluff shelved away and collapsed. The blasting powder planted earlier by Thurl Hampton had done its job as it was set off by Thurl in response to Fury's signal.

The avalanche came crashing down around the roadhouse. The men still inside the building must have known from the sound of the explosion what was about to happen, because they came boiling out like rats off a sinking ship. As they emerged, rifles began barking from the hillsides overlooking the canyon as the miners who had hidden themselves there opened up on the men who had made their lives miserable and tried to steal their hard-earned gold.

The Hellhounds never had a chance.

In those same frozen instants of time, J. D. took advantage of the sudden uproar and confusion and twisted around in Corey's grip. He fired, but the barrel of his gun was no longer pressed against J. D.'s head. The bullet went harmlessly past her. J. D.'s knee flashed up, burying itself in Corey's groin, and as the agony of the blow made him stagger, she jerked away from him and went diving to the ground.

Sullivan got off a shot that plucked at Joe Brackett's sleeve, but the big Irishman never got a chance for a second try. Joe's revolver blasted twice, the slugs driving into Sullivan's broad chest and knocking him backward in a lifeless heap. At the same time, Laidlaw was trying to draw a bead on Fury, but Fury darted to the side as the Australian fired. The Dragoon in Fury's hand boomed, its report all but lost in the cacophany of the avalanche. The heavy ball took Laidlaw in the midsection and doubled him over, but somehow the man stayed on his feet long enough to lift his gun for another shot.

Fury beat him to it.

This time the ball caught Laidlaw in the forehead, snapping his head back as it bored through his brain and erupted from the back of his head in a grisly shower of gray matter and bone fragments. Laidlaw folded up like a house of cards in a strong wind.

That left Will Corey.

The former teacher howled curses and tried to bring his gun to bear on J. D., who lay on the ground a few feet away. His face was contorted with hatred and madness. All of his schemes had come to nothing, all of his dreams had been

ripped away from him. But at least he could avenge himself
on J. D.

Fury and Joe fired at the same instant, and Corey was flung
backward by the impact of the slugs in his body. He landed
on his back, legs sprawled out and arms flung wide. For a
moment, he looked up at the sky so far above him, and his
mouth worked, but if any sound came out, it was lost in the
roar of the avalanche. Then his head fell to the side and his
eyes began to glaze over.

The mayor of Last Chance Canyon was dead.

A second later, a huge slab of rock weighing hundreds of
tons smashed down directly on the roadhouse, crushing it to
powder for all eternity. As the rocks continued to fall, Fury
ran forward, grabbed J. D.'s arm, and hauled her to her feet.
With his hand still grasping her arm, he led her toward the
center of the canyon at a dead run. Joe was right beside
them. There was no telling when a stray boulder might come
bounding toward them.

Once they were well clear of the avalanche, they stopped
and turned back to survey the aftermath of the awesome
destruction. The Hellhounds were all dead, some of them
shot down by the miners, the rest crushed by the falling
rocks. The roadhouse itself was nothing but a memory. A
huge cloud of dust rose into the late afternoon sky above
the canyon.

Fury, Joe, and J. D. were still standing there a few minutes later when the rest of the miners rode up, led by Ben
Hampton. Grinning broadly, Hampton said, "Looks like your
plan worked, John. We won't have to worry about the Hellhounds anymore."

J. D. turned and looked at Fury. "Plan?" she echoed.

"John came up with a good one," Joe told her. "There was
no gold strike in Frenchman's Gulch. That was just to make
the Hellhounds think we were on our own, so they'd come
out of their hole. We sent Thurl up to the top of the bluff to
set some charges of blasting powder so that when the time
came, we could take the gang by surprise." Joe laughed. "I'd

say they were surprised, all right."

"I could've been killed, you know," J. D. said to Fury.

He shrugged and smiled a little. "Seemed like you'd have a better chance with an avalanche than with Corey and that bunch."

A little shudder went through her. "I think you're right." She put a hand on his arm. "Thank you, John."

Before Fury could say anything, a shout went up from one of the miners. "Look!" he cried excitedly, pointing up at the cliff where Cougar Bluff had been. All of the overhanging ledge had collapsed, leaving a nearly perpendicular rock face.

And in the center of it, like it had been drawn there by some divine finger, was a long, gleaming golden streak.

In a matter of moments, men were swarming over the rubble of the avalanche, whooping in glee as they picked up nuggets the size of a man's thigh. The Hampton boys were among them, but Ben Hampton hung back and studied the vein that had been revealed by the explosion. He said, "Seems to me that's probably the other end of that ledge you uncovered on your claim, Joe. You got a legal right to follow it all the way up here."

Joe shook his head. "That's too much gold for one man, Ben," he said. "We'll all work it. There's enough ore there to make every miner in Last Chance Canyon a rich man."

A grin spread across Hampton's face. "You mean that, Joe?"

"I sure do."

Hampton nodded slowly. "Reckon there'll be a weddin', once Milo gets back on his feet. We'll buy us a big ol' farm, big enough for me and the boys and Milo and Nora, too. Things are goin' to be just fine now."

J. D. said, "And I'll build that store, just like Joe said. The finest one in all of San Francisco." She still had her hand on Fury's arm, and she looked up at him to ask, "What about you, John? What dream are you going to fulfill?"

Fury shrugged, thinking about Rachel Angelisi back in San Francisco. He wouldn't mind paying her another visit, maybe get to know her a little better, but then it would be time to move on again.

He settled for saying to J. D., "I don't know. Reckon we'll just have to wait and see."

Leaving the miners to their frantic work, Fury, Joe, and J. D. started back toward Joe's claim. Ben Hampton went with them and loaned J. D. Orville's horse. The youngest Hampton son could ride double with one of his brothers to get home later.

J. D. and Hampton rode a little ahead, and in a low voice, Joe said to Fury, "You still don't want your rightful share of the gold, do you?"

Fury grinned. "Being rich makes a man get all set in his ways sometimes. Don't reckon I want to risk it."

"Well, I'm sure as hell going to settle down," Joe said. "I'm tired of never having a place to call home."

Fury didn't say anything. Joe might believe what he was saying, but Fury had his doubts that things would work out that way. There was too much of the drifter in Joe Brackett for him to ever settle down for good. Fury knew that, knew it as well as he knew himself. One of these days, his path and Joe's might just cross again.

And as for not having a place to call home . . . well, Joe was wrong about that, too. From the Rio Grande to Canada, from the muddy waters of the Mississippi to the pounding waves of the Pacific, from the deserts to the forests to the mountains . . .

The West was John Fury's home.